D1374330

HANDS OF THE HEALER

The Christmas Emerald

ALLIE MARIE

This book is a work of fiction and does not represent real events.
Characters, names, places, and incidents are works of the author's
imagination and do not depict any real event or person living or dead.

HANDS OF THE HEALER
The Christmas Emerald
Book 4 of the True Colors Series
Copyright ©2018 by Allie Marie

Published by Nazzaro & Price Publishing
Published in the United States of America
ISBN: **1986708896**
ISBN-13: **978-1986708890**

DEDICATION

To Jack, the love of my life and the inspiration for any hero I can imagine.

CONTENTS

ACKNOWLEDGMENTS

I owe a world of gratitude to the many people who make it possible for me to fulfill my writing dreams. Thank you is not enough to say:

To my husband Jack, for your unwavering love and support.

To Tamara, for cheering me on. I love you, baby sister.

As always, to Sandi and Laura for your patience and diligence in reading my drafts—and then reading the many revisions.

To my editor Helen Brown Nazzaro and publisher/cover artist James Price for the continuing support, friendship, and assistance you always provide.

To Laura Somers Photography, for your assistance with the photo that enabled James to create yet another perfect cover. To Logan and Jack for being good sports and so patient during the photo shoots.

I am grateful to all the readers who enjoy my stories, especially Elizabeth, Fran, Kathy, Linda, Marty, Penny, and the ladies at the Windsor Book Club.

To other researchers of Antoine and Theotiste Paulint, the inspiration for Étienne and Clothiste in the <u>True Colors Series</u>. I created several colonial anecdotes based on family lore. One day, we shall all meet and celebrate our common ancestors, Catherine "Kitty" Wilson, Karen Fontaine, and Lonnie Smith, Jr! Thank you for the additional information on French "dit" names, Kitty.

Writing various scenes in Kirby's story required research and I obtained technical advice from many knowledgeable people. Any errors are all mine. I can't begin to adequately thank the following for their input:

To *mon ami* Stéphane Roche, whose assistance with the French language and all things French military prevented me from writing something that would have been lost in translation—or as in one case, a total *faux pas. Merci, ma "famille" française pour de nombreuses années d'amitié et d'amour.* Any mistakes are all mine.

To Ashley Schroeder, CAPT (ret) MC USN, for answering my many medical queries and for insight that enabled me to create Kirby's Naval physician persona.

To Carrie Hankes, Lauren Monarch, and historical reenactor Don Waldmiller for answering a plethora of questions about the colonial times in Yorktown. I made several visits to the American Revolution Museum at Yorktown, Virginia, to capture the essence of the period through their many displays and exhibits, including the Continental Army Encampment. I also referred many times to their website for information. You can find out more about the Siege at Yorktown at: https://www.historyisfun.org/.

Other resources used:
Reed, Adela Peltier, (1940). Memoirs of Antoine Paulint. Los Angeles, CA. San Encino Press
Online resources retrieved from:
https://ahec.armywarcollege.edu/trail/Redoubt10/index.cfm
http://www.francogene.com/quebec/ditnames.php

Author's note: When I began writing the True Colors Series, my original plans were for a trilogy based on the three colonial sisters and their lost jewels. As happens in fiction, characters can take on lives of their own. A young man, intended to be a minor background character, became a major figure when Louis appeared and his story needed to be told. With the restless ghosts already settled in the first three books, I needed a new twist to continue the saga. *Voila!* Kirby's time travel was born.

For fun, each of the chapters in *Hands of the Healer* are titled with songs that have something to do with time, midnight, or clocks. Enjoy!

PROLOGUE

Louis
Somewhere in time

I do not regret killing men on the battlefield. I was a soldier and it was my job. I had to kill a number of men in the call of duty.

But there is one death I cannot shake from my memory.

That night, I committed murder. It haunts me.

I pace the dark room. A few steps in any direction and I am face-to-face with a cold, dank wall.

I'm trapped—caged like a miserable animal.

Sometimes light appears through a small window in the wall. I race to see what is there.

But when I reach it, all is dark. My hands roam in mad desperation but I cannot find the casement.

Now the room spins.

It is always the same.

Total darkness surrounds me. The window will not reappear any time soon. I have scoured every inch of these barriers with my fingertips. Side to side. Top to bottom. Yet I cannot find a way out.

I never do.

When a brilliant yellow square gapes in the wall, light floods in, but I know if I look, I will see the same scene, the one I relive over and over. It will be the murder.

It always is.

But tonight. Tonight, the light of three short flashes appears in the wall. At first, I am reminded of gunfire the night I killed the soldiers.

But this is different, and that memory quickly fades. For the first time in centuries I feel a moment of peace.

A swirl of red, white, and blue sparks explodes through the opening and falls around me like snowflakes.

I hear my sisters' laughter.

Just as snow melts on warm ground, the sparks fade away, the laughter with it. I plunge into darkness again, and the spinning motion continues.

Does the room rotate around me, or do I spin head over heels? I cannot tell.

The spinning stops abruptly. I hear music and voices. Dazzling pinpoints of green light spring from a new gap, stunning hues dance along the walls around me. I see blurry images.

A boy's laughter fills my ears. My son?

His boyish voice sings out, "Lou-weeee!"

Why does my son call me by my given name instead of Papa?

I reach the window and see a small boy. He waves and disappears.

Come back! *I shout. My mouth moves but there is no sound. The words are only in my head.*

The window darkens as if shutters have been drawn. Once again, I plunge into blackness. The room whirls and I close my eyes. Behind my lids, tiny green sparkles explode in echoes of light instead of sound.

In desperation, I run my hands over the wall. I reach the corner and turn to the left. I repeat this all around the room until I am back where I started.

Or I think I am. How can I tell? Nothing changes.

A sudden burst of light pours through the small rectangle in the dark. I fling myself in front of it before it can leave me again.

The window has become a watery mirror. I see a man on the other side. He wears a redcoat uniform. The face stares back at me. At first, I think it is my face.

Am I looking at my own reflection?

Or is this the face of the one who will free me from my hell?

I can see him through the quivering opening. I motion the man closer. In tandem, we move our hands from side to side across the clear surface.

Then I push my hand forward—and my fingers plunge through the looking glass.

CHAPTER 1

"One Moment in Time"

Kirby
Portsmouth, Virginia, Present Day

Naval Lieutenant Commander Kirby Lawrence typed final notes in the chart, hit save, then closed the electronic medical records program before he shut his computer down. The monitor screen darkened. Stingy afternoon sun filtering through the small window to his right cast long shadows around his office. He yawned and leaned back in his chair, stretching tired shoulder muscles. Twisting his outstretched left hand until he could see his watch, he squinted at the LED.

Three o'clock.

He was now officially on leave. He'd been on duty almost twenty-four hours, with only three hours of broken sleep. At two-thirty in the morning, he had just dozed off when he was summoned to the OR to operate on a young sailor who suffered a fractured leg and heavy road rash in a motorcycle accident. After the surgery, Kirby had fallen asleep in his scrubs, managing another hour's rest before starting his morning rounds.

After checking in on his motorcyclist patient, still under heavy sedation, Kirby had just started routine medical rounds when another emergency came in. Three sailors aboard an aircraft carrier at the Norfolk Naval Shipyard were injured during a General Quarters Drill and were rushed to the Naval Medical Center Portsmouth. Formerly called the Portsmouth Naval Hospital and the oldest continuously running hospital in the Navy medical system, the facility saw its share of medical situations ranging from everyday illness to traumatic injuries.

As one member of the Gold Team on duty, Kirby had received the most critically-injured seaman, who had fallen to the deck below, striking several pipes along the way. The patient had a fractured scapula, broken femur, and crushed pelvis. The shoulder and thighbone were the least of the worries. The shattered pelvis and the potential resultant internal injuries were a challenge even to the skilled orthopedic surgeon and the other doctors attending to the patient. The team could not perform orthopedic surgery until they could identify the full extent of injuries and sources of any internal bleeding. The patient's blood pressure had plunged so low that he might not survive surgery. X-rays revealed one of the worst cases of a shattered pelvis and femur that Kirby had ever seen.

Except perhaps for his own. Kirby shifted and unconsciously rubbed his thigh. Almost two years ago he had suffered a nearly-identical trauma as the young sailor on the table. Ten days spent in a shock trauma unit and two weeks in critical care led to three months flat on his back with the equivalent of a medical Erector set extending from his body.

And he'd been the lucky one. One colleague lost his life, the other both legs.

An incoming text message pinged on his phone and he glanced at the number. His fiancée, Liana.

Going to be late for dinner. Got some last-minute things to do for the conference next week and traffic is already backing up on the interstate.

Kirby typed a response. *Rough day, with two emergency surgeries. How about I come over and we just order pizza?*

Liana answered quickly. *I don't know how late I'll be. It's a long drive and I'm sure you're tired. Just come over tomorrow after I close the shop. We'll chill out then.*

Kirby rolled his eyes skyward and stretched a kink from his neck. Thirty miles was not a long drive. But if the downtown tunnel was backed up with the usual Friday evening traffic, it could well turn into an hour-long commute. He tapped the keypad. *Yeah, maybe tomorrow is better. I'll go to the hospital to check on my newest patients before I head to your place.*

Liana's answer pinged immediately. *I thought you were going on leave. Did you cancel?*

Kirby sighed. As much as he would have preferred to oversee the care of the two sailors, military leave was not cancellable. He tapped: *No, you know I can't withdraw leave. I'm just going to check on them and turn them over to my team. See you tomorrow evening. Love you.*

It was nearly a minute before Liana answered. *Ok, gotta run.*

Kirby glared at the phone as the light faded from the screen. He almost wished he could take back the last two words of his text—words that were getting harder and harder to say.

Since he couldn't, he called the floor and checked in on the patient with the pelvic injury.

"He's hanging in, Doc," the nurse said. "Vitals are stable, breathing good. He's stirred a couple of times but went right back to sleep."

"Call me immediately if there are any complications," Kirby ordered.

"Will do, Doc. And get some rest yourself. Looks like you had quite a day."

"Yes, it has been. I'm gonna go home and crash, but I'll check on him throughout the night. If he can survive the next twelve hours, he might make it."

Kirby hung up after bidding the nurse good-night and punched the number 3 on his keypad. He had his favorite pizza place on his speed-dial. The Italian owner answered the phone with a cheerful "*Pronto.* This is Antonio. *Ciao*, Doc, *come va?*"

3

Antonio's accent always brought a grin to Kirby's face. "*Bene*, Antonio, I'm good."

"You wanna you usual pizza? Medium, peppers, onions, black olives?"

"Yep." *Pretty pathetic that you order pizza so often that Antonio recognizes you on caller ID and knows what you want.* Kirby pushed the thought aside and grabbed his briefcase and keys.

"To-a you house or to-a the hospital? Twenty minutes either way."

Kirby's apartment was not far from the medical center. "My place." Kirby glanced at his watch. "I should get there about the same time as the pizza. *Grazie*, Antonio."

***

In perfect synchronization, the delivery person drove up just as Kirby withdrew mail from his mailbox. As the young man brought the pizza to him, the tired doctor tucked the letters under his chin and fished for a twenty he had in his pocket. "Keep the change," he told the gangly young man with earphones dangling around his neck.

"Thanks, man." The pizza man saluted and stuffed the earphones in his ears as he shuffled back to his car.

Once inside the apartment, Kirby set the pizza and mail on his coffee table. He kicked off his shoes and unbuttoned his shirt as he headed to the kitchen for a beer from the fridge. He returned to the living room and plopped on the couch, sitting there with the bottle in his hand. He was too tired to unscrew the top.

His gaze fell on the pile of mail. The corner of a thick manila envelope jutted out and he pulled it from the heap. He recognized his Uncle Marion's scraggly handwriting. Kirby pinched the stuffed envelope between his fingers, then flipped it over to open the seal.

Maybe Uncle Marion sent some family tree information.

Kirby had become interested in his ancestry ever since he'd met the Dunbars, a local family with three mysterious properties in the historic Olde Towne district of Portsmouth. From previous talks with one of the owners, Terry Dunbar, and her genealogist boyfriend Kyle Avery, he'd learned about the significant French connection in her ancestry. He'd felt an immediate bond with the family that intensified as he met each member, but from the beginning the buildings had intrigued him the most. During his jogs, he had often felt drawn to run past the trio of former houses now containing family businesses.

His family heritage consisted of mostly English and Irish, as far as he knew. But ever since a party celebrating the opening of the B and B—when he'd seen a strange image in an antique mirror—he'd felt compelled to check further and had written to his uncle.

He pulled a stack of papers from the envelope. Held together by a huge clamp, one of the pages loosened and fell onto his lap. Kirby wasn't sure what he would learn when he read the contents, but he knew he somehow had a connection to the Dunbar family or their property.

Kirby's beer remained unopened and his pizza grew cold as he perused the information.

He sat bolt upright as he read aloud the last lines of his uncle's letter:

"Well, we're not just British with a touch of Italian. Hang on to your old *chapeau*, kiddo. Somewhere in some moment in time the ancestors mixed it up a bit. It looks like we might be damn Frenchies after all."

CHAPTER 2

"Good Times Bad Times"

After checking on the status of his patients Saturday morning, Kirby took care of some personal business before he arrived at his fiancée's apartment. Still exhausted from his marathon shift at the hospital, he'd fallen asleep on the couch while waiting for Liana to get home from work. Whatever time she'd come home, she'd left him sleeping.

Feeling a little more human after breakfast the next morning, Kirby flipped through the local news section of the Sunday paper. Liana sat across from him, reading the lifestyle segment. They drank coffee in silence, with only the occasional rustling of newspaper or clink of cup against saucer sending sound across the table.

"I see your *friends* from the café are in today's news." Liana's remark broke the blanket of quiet.

The edge in her voice when she said "friends" caused Kirby to frown. He lowered his page and looked over the top. "What'd you say, hon?"

She folded the newspaper in half and slid the section toward him. "Apparently those women at that French café you're so fond of have uncovered antique necklaces that they can trace back to ancestors from the Revolutionary War. There's a picture of the three of them together wearing their necklaces. Take a look at those stones. Individually, they are valuable but collectively they must be worth a small fortune." Liana topped off her coffee cup and set the pot on the trivet without offering to refill Kirby's. "I remember that gold cross with the sapphire stone, the one that woman wore when we were eating at the café. Do you remember her? What was her name? She bought our lunch that day."

Oh, hell no. Kirby had no idea whether the woman wore a gold cross or a string of seashells around her neck, but if he did, he wouldn't admit it. Liana would accuse him of looking at the woman's boobs instead of the jewelry. And mention her name? *Double hell no.* In Liana's eyes, that would qualify as having an affair.

"I think the family that owns the place is named Dunbar," Kirby answered, not looking at the photo. He still hadn't mentioned his uncle's letter to Liana and the fact that he may be connected to the women or the café in some way.

Liana nodded. "All three women are descendants of some French couple from colonial times. The article says one woman…" She craned her neck to read the print and then continued, "Stephanie Kincaid was doing ancestry, and her research led her to discover her family ties to the other two, as well as their connections to the old jewels. And to top it all off, they uncovered a skeleton to boot. Looking for skeletons in the closet is one thing. Finding one in the backyard is pretty creepy."

Kirby sighed and folded the paper, pushing it to the side. *No point in reading the paper now, is there, if you're going to tell me everything.* As he reached for the coffee pot, he said, "I remember the news coverage about Hurricane Abby. Old bones were uncovered under a tree that fell during the storm." He poured, and frowned into the less than full cup, wondering why Liana always left a small amount behind in the pot. *So that she wouldn't drink the last drop and have to make a new one?*

Liana nodded again as she nibbled a triangle of toast. "So,

one of the women, the one with the cross necklace with the sapphire, had DNA testing done which concluded the remains were not from a relative but apparently from some ancestor's second wife or something. Can you believe they even had the bones reburied in a cemetery? I wouldn't have wasted my money. Just plant them back in the ground where they came from."

Like you would do? Kirby swirled the last of the coffee in his cup. There was no point in discussing the matter with Liana. She wouldn't see the dignity or humanitarian aspect of such an act of kindness. She would only see the costs associated with it.

Better to change the subject.

He leaned toward her chair with a flirty grin and brushed a curl from her cheek. "I've got an idea. I could go with you to your conference in Richmond, just to get away. When we come back, you could close your shop early Friday. We can meet on the riverfront and walk around Olde Towne a bit before we check in at the inn."

Liana shook her head. She stood and rubbed her cheek as if washing away Kirby's caress. "You'd be bored stiff by Tuesday if you went with me. It's better if I go alone. I'll just be gone until Thursday. But as far as Olde Towne, I've seen everything there is to see in downtown Portsmouth. I don't know why you are so set on staying at that B and B Friday night anyway. I'd rather go down to the Outer Banks and spend the weekend in an oceanfront room. Now, I'd take off early if we were going there. But—we're not." Liana gathered her dishes and walked to the sink. "Besides, Christmas is coming up. Don't want to miss those early shoppers making my cash registers jingle all the way." She turned and headed down the hall, dancing a little jig as she hummed "Jingle Bells."

Over the rim of the cup, Kirby narrowed his eyes at Liana's back as he sipped the last of his cold coffee.

Have we ever really loved each other? Why don't we just call off this engagement?

***

Liana had trashed the morning paper before he'd had the chance to finish reading it, so Kirby stopped at the convenience store near his apartment. He purchased the last newspaper and returned to his car. Parked in front of the convenience store with the engine running to ward off the cold, he shuffled through the pages. Locating the section covering local news and events, he tossed the rest of the newspaper onto the passenger seat.

He drew his gaze to the article about the three women, their Bed and Breakfast called Clothiste's Inn, and the French café next door. Leaning back in his seat, he studied the two photos on the front page. One depicted a close-up photo of the three jewels Liana had drooled over—a white teardrop-shaped diamond, a red ruby heart, and a gold cross with a sapphire at the center. The other photo featured the three women together: the lawyer Terry Dunbar, the café owner Mary Jo Cooper, and the researcher Stephanie Kincaid.

He'd encountered Terry on several occasions over the last few weeks. He'd later met the rest of her family at the grand opening of Clothiste's Inn. He and Liana were scheduled to be among the first overnight guests at the quaint inn.

A sudden tingling sensation rippled through his left hand, radiating from the ring on his finger and up his arm to his shoulder. He glanced at the heirloom emerald ring he wore, turning the rim until the rectangular stone centered on his finger. The gold setting warmed his skin, an odd sensation that had occurred a number of times after he'd received the ring as a Christmas gift from his father. Since meeting the Dunbar family, the episodes increased in both frequency and intensity.

Flexing his fingers, Kirby perused the paragraphs that described how Stephanie Kincaid's ancestry search led her to Portsmouth and the discovery of her ties to a colonial family who once lived there. She met the two other women and together the trio uncovered their mysterious connections to each other as descendants of the same French Army officer and his French-Canadian wife.

The article continued with a description of the events after the recent storm. "When Hurricane Abby ripped through the area in September, the destructive storm damaged the Bed and Breakfast as well as the French café next door. In the aftermath, a construction crew discovered an old skeleton caught in the roots of a felled magnolia tree. Family records eventually led to the identity of the remains as well as the discovery of the three necklaces that belonged to three young sisters in the eighteenth century."

Now this is really getting interesting. Kirby flipped to the interior section to continue reading. The colonial girls were the daughters of Étienne and Clothiste de la Rocher. The parents' names mentioned in the article were also similar to some names listed in the family tree chart his uncle had recently sent. He straightened further at mention of a brother to the three sisters. *Louis de la Rocher.* He tapped the page with his ring finger. The emerald stone glowed, the gold metal vibrating and heating his skin to an uncomfortable temperature. He stiffened his fingers and jerked his arm to a full stretch, shaking his hand.

A loud rap on the driver's window startled him, and he angled his head to stare into the concerned eyes of an older black woman. She held a cup of steaming coffee in one hand. The sweet aroma of hazelnut creamer drifted to his nostrils as he rolled the window down.

"Are you all right, young man?" she asked. "I saw you bent over and was afraid you were ill."

"No, I'm fine. Thank you for checking. I just got involved with reading something in the newspaper."

"Well, I'm glad you are okay. You have a nice day now."

"Yes, ma'am. Thank you again."

The diminutive woman smiled, revealing perfect white teeth in her pleasant face. She entered the car parked beside his, and Kirby waved. He reached over the seat for his briefcase, realizing at the same time that he had left it at Liana's. He twisted back to a sitting position and drummed his fingers on the steering wheel. He dialed her number and when her answering machine kicked in, simply said, "Call you back in a little while."

He glanced, first at his ring, then the newspaper.

With a determined grip on the gearshift, he backed out of his parking space and headed toward the French café mentioned in the article.

Pâtisseries a la Carte seemed to be calling him for something other than French pastries.

CHAPTER 3

"Time Is on My Side"

Kirby drove the short distance from the convenience store to the street where three restored homes nestled behind a picket fence along the perimeter of the large lot. One building housed a law firm headed by Terry Dunbar. To its right rested the recently renovated B and B called Clothiste's Inn. Completing the trio, to the right of the B and B nestled the pleasant little café, *Pâtisseries a la Carte,* where he first met the dynamic attorney and her family.

He'd felt an inexplicable connection to Portsmouth—ever since writing a college thesis on the roles the city and Yorktown played in the American Revolution. After he'd been assigned to the medical center in Portsmouth, he'd moved to an apartment in the nearby historic district of Olde Towne just because of its connection to the colonial period.

Clothiste's Inn had intrigued him the moment he'd first seen it under renovation during one of his jogs. After that, he changed his running schedule to include going by the colonial-style building to observe the construction progress every week. He'd always paused for a moment to admire the huge old magnolia tree in the rear of the parking lot.

He would have said he had a morbid attraction to the tree, but brushed it off as fanciful.

After the destructive Category 2 Hurricane Abby roared through the area and toppled the beautiful old magnolia, workers discovered the old skeleton caught up in the roots. Kirby became convinced his fascination with the inn—and the tree—was more than a flight of fancy.

Autumn decorations in the windows and on doors promised the bounty of the upcoming Thanksgiving feast, with some American flags and "Thank you, Veterans" placards scattered among the fall foliage saluted the military holiday.

Kirby drove into the lot behind the businesses, where a small group of women gathered around a red Ford Fiesta parked a few spaces away. A diminutive black woman patted the hood, grinning from ear to ear. Kirby recognized her as the same lady with whom he had conversed at the 7-11. The three stars of the newspaper article he'd just read surrounded her, admiring the car. He parked a few spaces away and walked over.

Terry glanced up and waved. "Hello, Commander Lawrence," she called. "Come see Mrs. Belford's new Fiesta."

Kirby ambled toward the group. Mrs. Belford smiled and said, "I just saw the commander a few minutes ago." She traced her fingers over the mirror and said proudly, "I won this at my church. I've never had a new car before."

"Wow, that's nice," Kirby said with a smile. "Congratulations, ma'am."

"The Lord works in mysterious ways," Mrs. Belford said. Her face beamed, and she angled her eyes skyward, nodding.

"Yes, He does," Terry agreed. She hugged the older woman and helped her into the driver's seat. "I'm so happy for you."

"Thank you for everything, Miss Dunbar. Now once we go to court and get that awful Mr. O'Grady in jail, we will be all set."

"I'm sure he will go away for a long time, Mrs. Belford. The police are uncovering more evidence against him every day."

Mrs. Belford nodded and started the engine. With a wave,

she backed out and drove off.

"Poor Mrs. Belford." The shortest woman of the trio, Stephanie Kincaid, turned and spoke to Kirby. "She was swindled out of her vehicle by an unscrupulous car dealer but she's doing well now. Terry is helping her with her civil case and the car salesman is in jail on a host of felony charges." She extended her hand. "Nice to see you again, Commander."

"Thank you. Please call me Kirby, ladies," he said, smiling. He reached for her hand, startled by the small spark of static electricity that passed between them.

"Oh, my goodness." Stephanie smiled in return. "Kirby, you remember Mary Jo?"

"I do." A similar reaction occurred when he shook hands with the red-headed Mary Jo. A tall, striking woman with bright blue eyes, she stiffened at the small shock but said nothing.

Next, he shook hands with Terry. Sparks literally snapped between them.

Her eyes widened as she glanced at their hands. "Oh, my. That's not the first time that's happened to us, is it?"

The same thing happened with all three of them. Kirby ignored the thought swirling in his head. None of the women seemed fazed by the sparks. He said, "Terry, do you remember once asking me whether I had French blood?"

Terry nodded. "Yes, I do. You were jogging one day by the cemetery and we nearly bumped into each other."

Stephanie inched closer, a look of surprised interest crossing her features.

Kirby nodded and continued, "Well, I've always known of my English and Irish roots, even knew of one Italian grandmother in the line. But after I met you, I started digging around old family records and began bugging my relatives for information. My uncle sent me an old genealogy chart someone had once created. It turns out the ancestors I thought were English and Irish actually had a French connection as well, through one of my many great-grandfathers. Then I saw the newspaper article today."

Kirby resisted the urge to bring up the fact that his ring had warmed his finger to the point of discomfort while he held the newspaper. It was enough to have sparks fly. It was another thing to tell these women he was getting vibes from an heirloom ring.

He smiled. "The reporter mentioned a brother in the family. From my uncle's notes, I'm pretty sure I am a descendant of the same ancestors mentioned in the article."

"Let's go inside," Stephanie urged, pulling him toward the rear door of the café. "I want to hear more."

Mary Jo dug keys from her pocket, and said, "So do I. Now even I am curious to hear more about your ancestry. I only recently learned of my own connection, and I'm beginning to think everyone is a descendant of Clothiste and Étienne."

As Kirby followed, he shoved his hands in his pockets.

His ring vibrated to the point that it almost hummed.

CHAPTER 4

"Another Place Another Time"

"We're usually closed on Sundays, Kirby," Mary Jo explained as she opened the rear door of the café. "But I promised our nephew I'd open and let him raid the pastry trays after he rehearsed for a play he is in." She pushed the door open and flicked the wall switch.

Bright light flooded the stylish kitchen. Measuring cups and bowls lined pristine stainless-steel counters in anticipation of the next business day. The light aromas of cinnamon, chocolate, and baked goods lingered in the air. In swift and efficient moves, Mary Jo grabbed a coffee pot with one hand and reached for coffee filters with the other.

Stephanie pushed Kirby toward the dining area, shrugging off her coat and tossing it across the back of a chair. Kirby followed suit, and they both dropped into nearby chairs.

"This is so exciting," Stephanie said. She drew a small notepad from her purse. "We knew about the brother from our gho…from our family history."

Kirby caught her stumble but said nothing. *Was she about to say ghost—or ghosts?*

"You've met Kyle Avery, Terry's boyfriend, right?"

Stephanie asked.

"Yeah, we've met several times. I have his business card but haven't called yet. Now that I have the papers I've been waiting for, I was going to ask him to help me with some research."

"Oh, I'm sure he'd be glad to, as will I. Kyle's already made so much progress on Étienne and Clothiste's family tree. I'll finish explaining the relationships now. I'm descended from the youngest daughter Nicole, Mary Jo is from the middle girl Marie Josephé, and Terry from the eldest, Theresé."

"Hmm." Kirby placed his chin in his palm. "Interesting that their names are derivatives of the ancestors, but ours are not—if indeed I am one."

"So, you picked up on that too? It took me a while to figure that out when I first made the connections to the three sisters." Stephanie smiled. "Oddly enough, my middle name is Nicole. I don't know if Louis had a middle name. What is yours?"

"Daniel."

"Oh, pooh, I was hoping it would be Louis. That would be a perfect connection."

"Kirby Louis Lawrence would have been a mouthful."

"It would." Stephanie laughed. "I had always pronounced 'Louis' the same way you just did, 'Lou' with the 'iss' at the end. I had to get used to saying his name with the French pronunciation sounding like 'Louie.'"

Commotion and voices arose from the kitchen and Stephanie stood. "Sounds like the gang's all here. Let me give Mary Jo and Terry a hand. Would you like coffee or hot chocolate?"

"Coffee's fine," Kirby called as Stephanie rounded the glass display case toward the kitchen.

A young boy barged in from the kitchen area, dressed in the costume of a colonial drummer boy. He banged on a drum suspended from straps at his shoulders, bumping chairs and tables in his chaotic march. A girl about the same age, dressed in a colonial gown, followed on his heels. Both skidded to a halt in front of Kirby, and the drummer tapped out a steady ta-dum, ta-dum, ta-dum-dum-dum rhythm.

"Hello, Lou-weeee." The little boy named Tanner grinned at Kirby.

Kirby stiffened. Tanner had once called him by the same name, drawing out the syllables. It was the night of the costume party, and Kirby had dressed as a colonial soldier.

Tanner pressed closer, bumping Kirby's knee as he poised with the drumsticks above the rim. "I remember the drum roll you showed me. Watch!" He repeated the beats again, louder. A woman Kirby recognized as the boy's mother, Beth, bustled up, a harried expression on her face. She took the drumsticks from her son with one hand, and with the other lifted one of the straps holding the drum. The little boy raised his arms as she slid the instrument over his head.

"Aw, Mo-om." He stretched the name to two syllables.

"I'm so sorry," Beth said. With an apologetic smile, she nodded to Kirby. "They were rehearsing for a patriotic skit in honor of Veteran's Day, and I promised them treats if they did well. Tanner's reached the limits of his attention span, I'm afraid."

Kirby laughed and ruffled Tanner's hair. "I think I remember the same thing happened at the costume party for the grand opening of the inn." At the party, he'd met the unhappy young child dressed as a drummer, complaining that he preferred a zombie costume.

With a few convincing words about the importance of drummer boys during the Revolutionary War—thanks to research conducted when he was preparing his thesis—Kirby had cheered up the youngster and taught him a few drum rolls.

Tanner grabbed Kirby's hand and squinted at the emerald stone, replicating the actions he had made during the party. He ran his fingers around the metal. Voice heavy with skepticism, he repeated the same question he had asked Kirby at the party. "Are you sure this isn't a girl's ring?"

The little girl moved closer and tiptoed to peek over Tanner's shoulder.

"I'm sure I'm sure." Kirby laughed. "Tanner, do you remember I once told you someone in my family wore a ring like this a long time ago, but the metal part was lost?"

Tanner nodded. "Why does it always feel kinda hot?" Before Kirby could answer, the exuberant child swiveled on his heel and shouted, "Hi, Aunt Step-anie!" and bounded toward the woman carrying a tray of steaming mugs toward the table.

The little girl stood on tiptoes and kissed his cheek, whispering, "*Bonsoir, Louis*," before she charged after Tanner.

Kirby stared. *The kid spoke French?*

After greeting Stephanie, the children dashed toward the glass display rack to choose treats. She set the tray on an empty table. Sliding a mug in front of Kirby, she asked, "Kirby, may I see your ring?"

"Sure." He slipped the heirloom past his knuckles and dropped it into Stephanie's outstretched hand. He raised his mug to test the coffee.

"Does the metal part ever feel warm to you?" she asked.

Kirby inhaled steam and coughed. "Well…"

Stephanie interrupted, holding her hand palm up. "Let me backtrack before you answer. And prepare yourself for what you're about to hear. Earlier, when we were discussing Étienne and Clothiste's family, we told you how our necklaces were heirlooms that once belonged to their daughters."

Kirby nodded as Stephanie handed him back the ring. He replaced the warm frame on his finger.

"When we were interviewed, we withheld one aspect of our experiences from the reporter." She withdrew her cell phone from a back pocket and scrolled. She turned the phone around to show Kirby a picture of a man's antique gold ring with a flat surface and bent prongs where a stone had once been.

"At one time, this ring obviously held a rectangular jewel of some sort." She touched her fingers to the teardrop-shaped diamond at her throat. "All three of us—Terry, Mary Jo, and I—have noticed that our jewelry often turns warm against our skin, as if trying to tell us something. I know that sounds crazy, but it's true. We've just come to accept it as one of the many strange events that occur within this family. When the time is right, there is a lot more to explain. But there's something else I want to tell you about. We discovered an old satchel in the attic of the inn, full of letters. There were many references to the family members in the letters that enabled us to document the genealogy all the way back to the colonial times. This ring in my picture was also in the bag, wrapped in tissue. We believe it to be the base of an emerald ring given to the only son of Étienne and Clothiste as a Christmas gift."

Kirby glanced at the picture and said, "Can you enlarge it to be the same size as this one?"

"I think so." Stephanie slid her fingers across the screen and set the phone on the table. Kirby placed his flattened hand beside a life-size photo of the stone-less ring.

"This is incredible. I believe your stone could fit in the frame," she said in an amazed tone. "What do you know about your ring?"

Kirby shrugged. "It's been in the family for generations. I heard stories that the emerald was somehow dislodged from the original setting in the nineteenth century. My grandfather inherited only the stone from his father. He had a new setting created and gave it to my dad for a birthday gift. Dad, in turn, gave it to me for a Christmas present the year I turned twenty-one. Along with my first legal beer."

Stephanie laughed, mesmerizing Kirby with the engaging sound.

Genuine and spontaneous. Had Liana ever laughed like that? He racked his brain trying to remember the last time his fiancée had laughed without it being at someone's expense, until he realized Stephanie was still talking to him.

"Kirby?" Stephanie tapped his shoulder.

"Sorry, I was on a side trip but I'm back now," Kirby said with a shake of his head. "What did you say?"

"I said you made me laugh at your 'first legal beer' comment." She slipped into a chair opposite Kirby. "I'm an only child and I never dreamed when I started my family research that I would find more relatives than I ever thought possible. It is amazing the number of offspring that can come from one couple in two hundred or more years. I'd love to see your documents, to see if we can match up our ancestry."

"I'll get them. They're in my…" Kirby rose. He sat down with a chagrined snap of his fingers. He reached for his cell phone. "I keep forgetting. They're in my girlfriend's car. I've tried to call her a couple of times. She may be on her way to my place." As before, he poked the number keys and held the phone to his ear until Liana's voicemail kicked in. He said, "It's me again. Just wanted to know if you'll be coming over tonight. I left my briefcase at your place. Could you bring it if you're coming here?" He touched the end call key and put the phone in his pocket. He leaned back in the chair.

The two children, seated at a small table nearby, burst into a wild fit of giggles. Both Kirby and Stephanie laughed. He continued. "Well, I have a slew of notes my grandfather put together a long time ago. He wrote down the stories his grandfather passed on to him. He dreamed of putting them into a book but never did. My uncle, who is about twelve years younger than my father, sent them to me when I started digging into the family tree."

"That would be fantastic to see. We were so fortunate to find many documents, letters, and journals that provided details and proof. Most have been in Terry's family for generations."

"Before we go any further, can you explain who is related to whom here?" Kirby waved his hand around the room.

"It's a bit complicated. Terry, Mary Jo, and I are each descended from one of the three daughters of Étienne and Clothiste, which makes us technically—ninth cousins—or maybe tenth. I always need to look at the chart to be sure. I was already engaged to Terry's brother Gage when we learned about this. At first, he was scared, but we've convinced him we are so far apart in the gene pool it doesn't even count."

"I can imagine his reaction." Kirby smiled.

"Étienne and Clothiste are our seventh great-grandparents. Right now, I'm going through a series of letters from three

21

cousins who lived for a time in Portsmouth during the Civil War era. We are descended from these women, who were also direct descendants of Étienne and Clothiste's daughters. Much of the family history was obtained because one of the women had applied for DAR membership—Daughters of the American Revolution. Are you with me so far?" At Kirby's nod, Stephanie continued. "The work of those nineteenth-century relatives preserved a fantastic trail back to colonial America and even to France. We also know there was one brother, Louis, but there have only been brief mentions so far. It's Louis, spelled L-o-u-i-s but we are pretty sure it would have been pronounced the French way."

Lou-weeee? Kirby glanced at the table where the two kids sat. Tanner and the little girl had both pronounced the name like that. The girl scrambled from her chair and skipped over to the display case of desserts.

Kirby jutted his chin toward the glass pastry case. "Who is the little girl in the costume? Is she family too?"

Stephanie turned her gaze to the child, now standing in front of the case, hands on knees as she studied the desserts. She pointed a finger and Mary Jo removed a platter of éclairs.

"Oh, that's Norrie. She's the daughter of Terry's law partner, Sandi Cross."

"Does she speak French?"

Stephanie shrugged. "Not that I know of. Why?"

"I'm not sure." Kirby laughed. "I thought I might have heard her say something in French earlier."

"Well, here comes her mother. You can ask her yourself." Stephanie jutted her chin toward the big bay window.

Kirby glanced out in time to see a woman grab a small bag from the rear seat of a car and shut the door. She walked up the stairs toward the café door and stepped inside under the tinkling bell.

Sandi tossed the hood of her coat back and drew a scarf from her neck. Her gaze flickered around the room and landed on Kirby before she continued searching.

He sucked in a breath. She had to be the prettiest woman

he'd ever seen.

His next thought echoed over and over in his mind.

If only this was another time, another place.

CHAPTER 5

"Time After Time"

Cheers from the kids disrupted Kirby's concentration on the woman.

"Yay! Mama's here!" Norrie plopped her plate on the table, the half-eaten éclair dangling precariously over the edge. Tanner followed as she ran toward the woman, who stooped down with arms wide and swept the girl into a hug, stretching one arm to include the boy.

"How did the rehearsal go?" she asked. She peeled the kids from her embrace and stood to remove her coat. Kirby's gaze swept over the woman from heel to toe as she hung the coat on a rack near the door. She wore a plain white blouse tucked into form-fitting black slacks and he took in every curve before averting his eyes.

"We were the best," Norrie declared with confidence. She grabbed her mother's hand and pulled her toward the table that bore the lop-sided éclair.

Kirby was so distracted, Stephanie left the table and returned with a plate of pastries and a pot of fresh coffee. He was completely unaware she had spoken until she tapped his shoulder.

"Are you on another side trip?" she asked, a dimple appearing as she grinned.

Kirby shook his head. "I guess my mind is wandering a lot today. I'm sorry, what were you saying?"

"I asked if you would like more coffee. Or can I get you a glass of tea instead?"

"More coffee would be great. I don't think I had enough to jumpstart my day." *Thanks again, Liana.*

Stephanie filled the cup again and said, "From the little bit you've told me, not to mention those telltale sparks when we shake hands—which you have noticed, right?"

Kirby nodded, rubbing his palm on his thigh. *Oh, yeah.*

"Well, for that reason alone, I would not be surprised to find out we are related. The same thing happened to me when I initially met the family members. First Terry, then Gage, then their mother Joan."

Kirby smiled as he lifted the coffee cup. "Maybe I'm going to need something a bit stronger to get through all of this."

Stephanie laughed and continued. "We keep finding distant relatives who are also tracing their family trees back to these same roots. One lady, her name is Catherine, is in Texas. Another, Karen, lives in Massachusetts. And we've even discovered Lonnie, a teenaged ancestry sleuth from Pennsylvania, who contacted us for info. None of us have met in person yet, but we've picked up so many clues from each other's research, and I think we've contributed a bit to their records. Kyle and I have also been weeding through tons of records and online data. He's writing a book on ancestry research and he is using the Dunbar family tree as an example. It's fascinating, and they have a rich history. And when they took Mary Jo in as a foster child, they had no idea she was a distant relation as well. One thing about this family. If you think it was hectic today, wait until the whole gang gets together. Big, noisy—and full of love."

"Terry's law partner? Is she related?" Kirby could not prevent his gaze from darting in Sandi's direction. *Too bad she's already married.* He inwardly shook his head. *And you're engaged, jackass.*

"Sandi? No, they were roommates in law school and just recently opened their partnership."

"I see." Kirby glanced at his watch. "Hey, listen, I've got to run. I'll try to get my papers tonight. My fiancée leaves for Richmond tomorrow, otherwise I won't see her until she returns later in the week. I think you already know we'll be staying at the inn for the weekend."

"Yep, you'll be our first official guests." Stephanie smiled. "We're so proud of Clothiste's Inn. Mary Jo's fiancé Chase did the restoration on all the buildings and he's done a fantastic job of capturing the colonial flavor of the B and B. Did you know that the inn was originally a house owned by Terry's family? It has a lot of history, far more than what the newspaper article revealed. Some of it is dark. I hope you are ready to find out everything."

"Ever since I suspected there may be a family link, that inn stuck in my craw and I've looked for answers. The sooner I find them, the better. I think I'll go now to get my briefcase, so I don't have to wait until Liana returns. How can I get my papers to you tomorrow?"

"You can leave them here with Mary Jo, or at Terry's office if the café is closed. Either one will get them to me. Kyle and I are off to research some stuff in Richmond Tuesday. In the journals and letters that I'm going through now, we've found out about a little girl from there who was visiting Portsmouth and went missing in the mid-eighteen-hundreds."

Kirby reached for his wallet and Stephanie shook her head. "It's on me, Kirby."

After exchanging goodbyes, Kirby weaved through the maze of small tables and ice cream parlor sets toward the door. Terry, leaning on the table where the gorgeous woman sat with Norrie and Tanner, waved him over.

"Kirby, I'd like you to meet my law partner, Sandi Cross. You've already met her daughter, Norrie. And you're an orthopedic surgeon at the Naval Hospital...oops, I still call it that from my father's days there. I meant the Naval Medical

Center Portsmouth. Is that right?"

"Yes, to both." Kirby accepted Sandi's extended hand and looked into eyes the color of a gray-green sea. "It's a pleasure…" they said in unison and broke into laughter.

"It is nice to meet you, Sandi," Kirby continued. "Terry, I'm sorry to rush, but I'm heading to my…to the beach to pick up my ancestry stuff for Stephanie and Kyle. She said I could leave them here or at your office tomorrow."

Kirby reached for his coat. *Now why did I stumble over saying "fiancée" just then?*

Terry smiled and waved, "No problem. Looking forward to seeing where this is all headed and if we come from the same ancestors."

Kirby returned the wave and the little bell tinkled overhead as he opened the door, then stepped into the chilly afternoon. The waning sun cast long shadows over the buildings. A gust of cold wind scattered crisp leaves across the pavement, scratchy noises rising and falling with the wind.

He cinched his jacket tighter and called Liana's phone. It wasn't like her to be out of touch for such a long time. He glanced at his watch. Four-thirty. He could get through the downtown tunnel and to her townhouse in less than half an hour. There were always the two chances—slim and unlikely—that she had noticed his briefcase and would bring it to him.

Lou-weee! The haunting voice whispered over the crunch of dried brown foliage. Kirby glanced over his shoulder to see if one of the kids had called to him.

Lou-weee! The second syllable ended on a muffled cry.

Empty streets surrounded him.

Kirby jumped behind the wheel of his car, rolling the window down to listen. A few leaves swirled and scratched along on the sidewalk, but he did not hear anything else. A chill ran down his spine and he blasted the heater. The engine, still warm enough from his earlier ride, enabled the heat to kick in quickly.

But warmth eluded him.

He glanced once at the café before flipping the turn

27

indicator. The signal clacked in time to the haunting tune of Cyndi Lauper's "Time after Time" playing on the radio.

***

Sandi Cross scooted to the window and peeked from behind the curtain in time to see Kirby enter his car and drive away.

"Oh my gosh, I've just fallen in love! Who is that gorgeous hunk?" She nearly backed into Terry, who had come behind her to peer out as well.

"Cool your jets, partner, he's engaged," Terry said.

"Aw, shit," Sandi answered with a slump of the shoulders.

A chorus of "oh-oh" resounded from the kids at the table. "Mommy said a bad word," Norrie said. "She owes me twenty-five cents." She and Tanner burst into giggles.

"I meant pooh, I meant pooh," Sandi hastened to interject. "Eat your treats."

In an aside to Terry, she added, "My daughter has become the swear word enforcer. I have to pay a quarter every time I slip up."

"We went through that with Tanner." Terry laughed. "He bought a 'Happy Meal' with his proceeds."

"Hmmm. She's well on her way to a full-course dinner at the Bier Haus. So...the doctor is engaged, huh? Darn. The good ones are always taken."

"Think you're ever gonna start dating again, Sandi?" Terry drew her law partner by the arm and steered her back to the table.

"I don't know, Terry. After getting through law school, then slaving at the Forrest firm before setting up practice with you, I haven't had time to think about dating again. And it took me such a long time to put the whole debacle with Norrie's father behind me."

"Well, that's one thing over and done with. Give it time. Someone will come along."

"And that's something I have a lot of—time." Sandi

glanced toward her daughter and smiled.

The Naval doctor's handsome face flashed before her eyes and she sighed.

Another place, another time, and things might have been different.

CHAPTER 6

"Time in a Bottle"

Washed-out dusk had settled into a starless black night by the time Kirby pulled in front of Liana's townhouse. He glared at the unfamiliar vehicle taking up the spot beside hers where he normally parked. Liana only had the two spaces assigned to her home in the townhouse complex. He'd have to find a place along the street. Vehicles filled every available place as far as he could see. He drove past, finding an empty space on a side street two blocks away. He got out of his vehicle and hit the pavement in a steady jog.

Fingers of a frosty wind spiraled down his collar, and he hunched in his coat, shivering. The bitter cold sliced across his thighs, shooting icy pains through his scars. Already, the cold affected his gait, causing the heel of his bad leg to scrape the sidewalk with every other step.

His bad leg. The leg he nearly lost in Afghanistan in a horrific accident almost two years earlier. The leg that Liana could not look at. He was less than perfect in her eyes now, and while she never said as much, her averted eyes told him more than enough.

The even-louder messages he should have paid more

attention to came from the times when she simply closed her eyes whenever he undressed near her. Even though his injuries had left one leg mangled and scarred, it had not affected his sex life. However, Liana was too often fast asleep when he joined her in bed.

It had long been over for her.

It was finally over for him.

I need to tell her tonight.

He strode up the driveway, dialing her phone so he would not startle her coming in, something she had always insisted he do. As he passed the strange black SUV parked beside hers, a muffled ring from inside matched the ringtone of her cell playing in his ear. He glanced in the driver's window. A cell phone shimmied on the passenger's seat, the face lighting up. He hit the disconnect button and the phone went dark.

Kirby frowned, his stomach dropping with an uneasy thud. Liana's cell was almost as much of an appendage as her very hands. He unlocked the townhouse door and leaving it ajar, stepped into the dim foyer. Light emanated from a room at the far end of the hall. His foot kicked something, and he peered down. Liana's black stiletto skidded into its mate and flipped onto its side.

Soft material wadded under his next step. Kirby lifted his foot and bent to pick up the white cotton blouse Liana had been wearing that morning when he left. Another lump followed about two steps further. Contents of Liana's purse spilled on the floor.

An uneasy twitch struck Kirby under his ribs. The meticulous Liana was not one to toss her clothes carelessly. He recalled the vicious attack that Terry had suffered at the hands of the crazed car dealer O'Grady. The twitchy feeling radiated upwards, sending tiny shockwaves of concern to his scalp.

Was Liana all right?

He held the shirt between his thumb and forefinger and used his ring finger to find the light switch. Startled by the appearance of a silhouette in the open doorway twenty feet away, Kirby froze in place, free hand curled into a fist. An eerie

31

shadow loomed across the walls as the person neared the bedroom door.

"Milk and sugar, Spencer?" A stark-naked Liana called over her shoulder as she emerged from the bedroom.

"Just milk," a lazy voice drawled from the room. "You're all the sugar I need."

Liana threw back her head and laughed, her perfect surgery-enhanced breasts jiggling as she waltzed down the hall toward the kitchen.

Kirby switched the light and Liana shrieked, one hand flying upward to cover her breasts and one down to cover her crotch as light flooded the hall.

"Kirby!"

Footsteps thumped the floor and an equally undressed man stepped to the bedroom door. "What the fuck is going on here?" he shouted, his hands cupping his genitals.

"I'd say all the fucking occurred before I got here." Kirby raked his gaze over Spencer's chiseled body and perfect, unscarred legs, then back to Liana. "I see you're both dressed for the occasion."

"Who the hell are you?" Spencer demanded.

Kirby ignored the query from Liana's lover and stepped closer to Liana. His jaw tightened, threatening to send his teeth crashing through his gums. He'd often wondered what he would do if he ever encountered this exact situation, expecting rage so furious that he would probably punch Liana in her face before turning his fists to her lover. He balled his hands, one white-knuckled fist locked on the blouse he still held. Would he risk his surgeon's hands in revenge?

He was about to find out.

"Kirby, what are you doing here?" Liana backed into the kitchen and grabbed a dishtowel to cover her chest. She snapped another from the counter and held it lower.

Kirby remained in place, gaze locked on Liana. A gust of wind blew the front door wide open, sending a few dried leaves scattering in the foyer. The wintery blast sailed inside, reaching his already-frozen earlobes.

Weather, he realized, was not the only thing that could turn a man's body cold. Shock, hate, and fury could turn a man's mind—and heart—to ice. Jaws taut, he stared. Liana averted her eyes first.

"Will you shut the damn door?" She shivered. "It's freezing and you're giving my neighbors a thrill."

Ignoring the request, Kirby said, "I've been trying to call you for hours, but since your phone is still on the seat of dickwad's car, I'd say you've been engaged in a marathon of screwing." Although his ears tingled from the cold, anger radiated from his lower body, creating a ring of heat along his neck. If the situation hadn't been so bleak, he would have laughed at the inane realization that he was hot under the collar.

"Please, Kirby, this is not what you think. This means nothing to me." Liana's voice ended in a squeak.

"Hey, wait a minute, what do you mean by that?" Spencer sputtered as he stepped in the hallway.

Eyes still directed at Liana, Kirby raised his arm and pointed at Spencer. "Don't move, don't speak," he warned, keeping the other man in his peripheral vision as he stared Liana down. "I'm deciding whether or not it's worth my time to break your fucking neck, but I'll take any reason to put it in the worthwhile category." Kirby caught the movement of the man slipping back into the bedroom. His glare burned through Liana.

"Kirby, please let me get some clothes on and we can talk about this." The fluorescent kitchen lights showed the lines in Liana's pinched face, thick smears of mascara dotting her skin. Her hair spilled from her normally perfect French twist, sticking out in scraggly spikes.

He held the shirt toward her. She reached for it and he let it fall a fraction of an inch from her fingertips, as he spat, "You sorry bitch."

"Oh, screw you, asshole." Liana picked the shirt up, shrugged into the sleeves and secured one button, tossing her hair and settling into a combative stance.

"Well, the wind has obviously returned to your sails," Kirby said. "There's the Liana I know and love so well. Too bad we aren't already married—I'd be telling you we're getting a divorce. As it is, the engagement's off."

"As far as I'm concerned, it's been off for months." She deliberately let her gaze drift to Kirby's bad leg.

Kirby narrowed his eyes and shoved his fists into his coat pockets. The sudden urge to grab her throat and press her windpipe until she turned blue crossed his mind and disappeared as quickly as it arrived. God knows, he'd never hurt a woman in his life. And he used his hands to heal people, not hurt. But the temptation was so—passionate. *Is that what "in the heat of passion" meant?*

Spencer emerged from the bedroom, dressed in slacks but shirtless. He carried shoes in one hand and stooped to snatch a blue chambray shirt from the floor nearest the bedroom. He strode down the hall and stopped two feet from Kirby. "I'm sorry, man, I didn't know she was seeing anyone."

"Try engaged." Kirby shrugged and moved to the side to let him pass.

"Where are you going, Spencer?" Liana stepped from the kitchen doorway and clutched his arm.

"As far from you as I can get. I don't poach in another man's territory." Spencer shook her hand loose and slid his arm into a sleeve, continuing toward the living room as he repeated the gesture with his other arm. He tossed his shoes on the ground, slipped his feet inside, grabbed a coat from a chair and stormed out the door.

"Well, that makes two of us." Kirby turned on his heel and followed Spencer.

"That's all?" Liana raced to his side and grabbed his arm. "That's all you have to say for almost three years together? Please don't go, Kirby, let's talk."

This woman is a freaking Jekyll and Hyde. He shook her hand free. "Yes, Liana, that's all I have to say."

He snagged Liana's car keys from the table. "I'm getting my briefcase out of your car and then I'm leaving for good. Keep the ring."

The flick to the back of his head told Kirby Liana had sent the ring sailing in his direction. It bounced and pinged through the open doorway onto the dark sidewalk. Spencer pealed from the driveway and sped away, before hitting the brakes and reversing. He got out and walked to the edge of the curb, tossing Liana's phone in the grass. He raced back to the driver's seat and pealed tires in his rapid getaway.

Not bothering to close the door, Kirby stood on the steps and brushed the unlock button on Liana's key fob. After it beeped and the car interior lighted, he tossed it behind him through the open doorway. It landed with a dull thud and skittered further inside. He fumbled for the car door handle and snatched his briefcase from the seat.

"Kirby, come back," Liana shouted. She stepped to the threshold.

Kirby swiveled on one heel and faced her. "Liana, go back inside and quit making a fool of yourself. It's over and you know it."

"You bastard. I hate you." Liana reached behind her and flung her hand toward Kirby. He took one step backward as a heavy crystal dish sailed his way. It arced and struck his bad leg before falling to the pavement with a shatter.

Kirby patted his thigh. "Titanium," he said and turned away.

***

So much on autopilot that he didn't remember most of the drive home, Kirby arrived at the parking lot to his apartment and pulled into his assigned space. He'd replayed the whole scene at Liana's over and over in his mind, leaving him unable to recall whether he passed any other vehicles on the interstate, or whether he had even stopped at traffic lights. He hefted the twelve-pack of Michelob he'd picked up at the convenience store—the only thing he really remembered doing—and trudged through the cold night to his door.

He wasn't a drinking man. An occasional beer or glass of wine at dinner was usually more than enough, as he preferred to keep a clear head for any medical situation he might deal with.

Plunking the box on his coffee table, Kirby shrugged out of his coat and went to the kitchen. He stood for three full minutes in front of the refrigerator door, unable to concentrate on the contents long enough to think of a meal.

He slammed the door shut, kicked off his shoes and plopped on the couch.

How long had it been going on? He'd always suspected that if one of them ever had an affair, it would be Liana.

She'd changed after his injury. Not right away. She had been a doting fiancée during his recovery and rehab.

He turned the top on a bottle and swigged half the contents before plunking it down.

Once he was transferred stateside, Liana had stayed by his side for the first two months of his recuperation. She brought the medical staff platters of cookies and cakes—store-bought, of course—and always arrived dressed to the nines. She'd craved the attention she'd gotten from the hospital staff. Even his injured colleagues had occasion to see past their pain and anguish to admire her good looks.

As rehab wore on, Liana's visitations dropped to three times a week. Soon she reduced her visits to once a week. When he came home, she moved a few things to his place, and stayed on occasional weekends.

Kirby guzzled the rest of the beer and sent the bottle on a wobbly roll toward the wall. He lined five more bottles on the table and popped the tops in succession. He twisted each bottle until the labels lined up in perfect formation with the first.

Tonight, he was a drinking man.

CHAPTER 7

"Only Time Will Tell"

Sprawled face down on the couch, Kirby opened one eye. Bright sunlight seeped through a crack in the blinds. He had fully expected to wake up with a hangover, a hangover he deserved, if the bottles littering the table and floor were any indication. He'd more than fueled the probability by downing one after the other in a last-ditch effort to forget the events of the encounter with Liana.

The break-up had taken less of a toll than he had anticipated. Maybe he hadn't realized his feelings for Liana had been slowly dying in the last few months—probably longer, if he was honest with himself. Still, it *had* been a shock to see her come from her bedroom in the nude, especially after he encountered her lover in the same state.

At least he hadn't caught them in the act of screwing.

Kirby eased into a sitting position, prepared for the onslaught of daggers to shoot through his temples. Surprisingly, his head was fine. He leaned his elbows on his knees, swallowing to get past the angora sweater that seemed to fill his throat. He counted the discarded bottles scattered around the coffee table. Eight empties, one half-full, one open but still full. He shook his head.

What one woman can do to your heart, your mind, and your soul.

By that count, he should have a rip-roaring headache. He didn't remember drinking so many beers. After he'd downed two in rapid succession, he'd spent a full minute wallowing in self-pity before guzzling two more. He ran his hands across scratchy stubble on his jaw and then dragged his fingers through his hair. He might not have a hang-over, but he still felt like shit.

His stomach rumbled. When had he eaten last? A little toast yesterday morning before he checked on his patients; some French apple pastry thing at the café. That was it.

He glanced at his watch. Noon! He jumped to his feet too fast, swaying as the blood rushed from his head. Or maybe it was the start of a splendid hangover after all. He swallowed past the angora and took a deep breath through his nose. An intermittent chirp, low and far away, signaled that his cell phone was on its last leg.

Kirby shuffled toward the fading sound with slow, cautious steps, and located the dying phone in a jacket pocket. His charger was—*where?* He held his hand to his forehead to ease the abrupt pain that pierced his temple. Stumbling to the kitchen counter where he normally recharged the phone, he stared at the empty outlet. He drummed his fingers but stopped immediately. To his aching head the strumming resembled a herd of stampeding elephants.

The charger was probably in his briefcase—in his car. He debated whether to get it or just let the damn phone die. Even though he was on leave, he wanted staff to contact him if the need arose. And he wanted to check on the condition of the two newest patients.

First things first. Coffee. He opened the cabinet to an empty canister. *Damn!* He'd forgotten to buy a new supply. Slamming the door shut, wincing at the gunshot-like crack reverberating in his ears he said aloud, "Get your shit together, Lawrence."

Kirby raked his hands across the stubble irritating his neck. He'd take a shower and clean up before heading to *Pâtisseries a la Carte.* There was also the reservation at Clothiste's Inn that needed cancelling.

One last tweet signaled the final death knell for his cell phone. Grumbling, he fished his keys from the clutter on his coffee table and shuffled to the door to retrieve his briefcase and find his charger.

***

Kirby felt more human after the shower and shave, not to mention the three extra-strength aspirin he'd swallowed dry.

His phone had charged enough to allow him to check in on his patients. The motorcycle crash victim was out of bed and hobbling on crutches. The other, more critically-injured patient had experienced a restless night and required an adjustment to the external fixator, the metal contraption acting as a stabilizing framework to holding the broken bones in place. Kirby knew well the discomfort of the device. Metal screws or pins were inserted into bones, and projected out of the skin, where they were attached to bars outside the skin.

"He's black and blue from the back of his head to his heels. He was doing well when I checked on him about a half hour ago," Lt. Commander Murphy O'Shea, another member of the Gold Team, relayed. "He was awake and able to see his mom for a few minutes. She arrived from Idaho this morning and I think that helped him tremendously. He's asleep now."

Kirby jotted some notes and told Murphy he'd check on the sailor after he grabbed some lunch.

"Um...aren't you on leave, partner?"

"And your point is, Murph?"

"Yeah, I know, man. I'd be doing the same." The two doctors exchanged goodbyes and hung up.

A spattering of snowflakes swirled as Kirby headed toward the café. He glanced toward the ominous clouds overhead. He hadn't bothered to check the weather reports the entire weekend and had no idea whether a storm was brewing or if this was just a flurry.

His phone vibrated with an incoming text, and he waited until he had parked in the rear of *Pâtisseries a la Carte* before looking at the incoming number.

Liana. *Shit.* Kirby's thumb hovered on the delete button, then he shook his head and opened the message.

I'm sorry. Can we talk? I didn't leave for my conference yet.

Kirby shook his head again and rolled his eyes skyward as he grabbed his briefcase and got out of the car. He poked the keypad with angry jabs. *Nothing to talk about.*

Her swift reply. *Bastard.*

Kirby slammed the car door and spelled out "B-i-t-c-h", but deleted the word, leaving no evidence that Liana could turn against him. Teeth clenched, he gripped the handle of his briefcase and stormed along the big walk-around porch to the entrance. The scent of baking bread drifted across the crisp air. He stepped inside the café, the bell over the door jangling merrily as the door opened and closed.

Diners occupied every seat in the small dining room. He scowled and glanced around, eying one of the ice cream parlor sets tucked near the bay window, where a man and woman rose from their chairs and walked to the glass counter.

Stephanie Kincaid bustled from the kitchen area, carrying a tray bearing steaming bowls of soup. She set them before four guests at a large square table, then glided to the register to take the payment from the couple waiting at the counter. Kirby could not hear the exchange, but she laughed, the sound as pleasant as the tinkling bells on the entry. She handed the couple a small gray bag displaying the café logo on the front. When she spotted Kirby, she waved and with a sweep of her hand, motioned toward the now-vacated table as she picked up dishes.

"Ah, you're back," she smiled. One look at his face and her bright expression turned to one of concern. "Are you all right?" she asked, blue eyes searching his.

Kirby shook his head, as if the act would shake the scowl pinching his features. His face relaxed. It was hard to stay in a black mood around Stephanie. He smiled. "Thanks, but I'm okay. Did you know it's snowing?"

"Really?" Stephanie peered through the curtains and shook her head. "Pooh. It's stopped already. The forecast wasn't calling for snow in this area until this weekend. I'll get you a menu."

"Thanks. And a cup of coffee, please," Kirby called to her retreating figure.

Several tables of diners emptied at about the same time and gathered around the glass case displaying the day's pastries. A small crone of a woman peered over the counter and took their orders, bagging them in shiny gray bags or boxes. Kirby recognized the tiny woman. He'd been introduced to Hannah once before, at the costume party where he'd met other members of the Dunbar family. The wizened old woman wore her hair in short spikes, and sported a bright yellow tee-shirt that said, "Don't needle me, you knit-wit."

Stephanie returned with a menu tucked under her arm, a coffee cup in one hand, and a coffee pot in the other.

"Fresh-brewed," she said as she poured. "Are you and your fiancée ready for the weekend at the inn?"

Kirby grimaced. "We broke up last night. I guess I need to cancel."

"Oh, no, I'm so sorry to hear that. Is there anything I can do?"

"No, I'm fine, really. It's been coming for a while, I guess."

"Well, if you'd like, I can take care of the cancellation for you at the register."

Kirby nodded. "Thanks." After a quick glance at the menu, he selected chicken rice soup and a BLT on a croissant. The lunch crowd thinned out and the last guests left, leaving Kirby as the only diner. He pulled his Uncle Marion's envelope from the briefcase. When Stephanie brought his food, he motioned toward the brown packet.

"When you have a moment, I wanted to show you the family tree my uncle wrote up which mentions those twins with the French names."

Stephanie clapped her hands. "I can't wait to look through

41

them." She glanced at her watch, then the door. "We close at two. I just need to get the last of the tables cleared before Hannah fires me for slacking off."

"Heard that and I will." Hannah's gravelly voice muffled through the glass of the display case as she moved plates around.

"She's got her head surrounded in glass and can still hear a pin drop at fifty feet."

"But she's adorable," Kirby said with a wink.

"Free dessert for the doc," Hannah called when she straightened. "The man has impeccable judgment."

"Slick move, Lieutenant Commander Lawrence. You have a friend for life," Stephanie said. She giggled as she gathered dishes from the tables.

***

"Finally finished." Stephanie dropped in the chair opposite Kirby, setting a coffee cup on the table.

Kirby leaned back and patted his stomach. "Man, that soup was great. Tasted like my grandma used to make. Can I get a bowl to take out?"

"Sure. That soup is Hannah's specialty," Stephanie said. "Mary Jo often creates gourmet specialties, but on days with weather like this, everyone seems to want good old-fashioned home-style foods."

"Yep." Kirby leaned toward Stephanie and tapped his finger on a chart from the packet. "My uncle improvised a hand-drawn family tree based on information he gathered years ago. He became interested in genealogy when he spent a summer with his Italian grandmother's family in Italy. My dad isn't into the ancestry stuff so much, other than the history behind the ring that says it's been passed down to the oldest son for a number of generations." Kirby twisted his hand, so the ring faced toward Stephanie. Mindful of the sudden flow of warmth emanating from the metal, he tapped his finger to a name.

"Uncle Marion traced back as far as eighteen-twelve, to a son born to a man named Phillip Lawrence and his wife, whom we only have recorded by the first name of Sadie. But they had three children, a son Louis, and boy and girl twins born two years later." Kirby kept his gaze on Stephanie's face, seeing her eyes widen as she looked at the names. She turned her gaze to him.

"The twins were named Étienne and Clothiste!"

Kirby nodded. "Apparently no one paid any attention to researching anything about the twins, so I can't provide any information on them. My direct line descends from the brother who was christened Louis but who later became Lewis Lawrence, spelled L-E-W-I-S. At some point, someone apparently anglicized the spelling of his name."

He poured coffee and hovered the pot over Stephanie's cup. She shook her head, absorbed in the written notes as she ran fingers along names on the chart.

"The twins do have unusual names for an Irish family, that's for sure. But you have no other documentation for French relatives?"

"Nope. My records only go back to Lewis Lawrence, who came to America around the time of the potato famine. As far as I could tell, Lewis' father died young in Ireland, and the mother brought Lewis and the twins to New England. She eventually remarried. Lewis had a son, Daniel Patrick, who served with the Union Army in New Hampshire. He received a pension, and Uncle Marion located the records for that. Daniel and his wife Lauralee lived until well in their nineties, and they kept pretty meticulous records for the times."

Stephanie cupped her chin with her hand. "Some of the Dunbar records were preserved because of documentation needed for Civil War pensions. Also, because of those pension records, one of my great-great-grandmothers was able to prove her connections to Étienne and his service during the Revolutionary War as part of her application to the Daughters of the American Revolution." She looked up. "Kirby, can I look through your records after I return from Richmond tomorrow? I'm right in the middle of a series of family journals I'm cataloguing. I think I may have mentioned that a little girl in the family from Richmond went missing here in Portsmouth around the early eighteen-sixties, but so far, I haven't found any record of her return. The journal entries are heart-wrenching, so I am kind of focused on finding out about the child."

"Take the whole package. There are too many names for me to sort through, and I have to admit, it's really not my thing."

"Well, I will take good care of everything and I'll return as soon as I can," Stephanie promised. She picked up the envelope as she handed Kirby his bill.

"Everything is a photocopy of Uncle Marion's originals, so nothing to return. I guess I better take the soup and head out. I'm going to visit some patients in the hospital and then go home." Kirby reached in his back pocket for his wallet and handed his debit card to Stephanie.

She headed toward the cash register, calling over her shoulder, "Oh, and I'll cancel your reservation for the inn now."

Kirby froze in place. The ring burned against his skin. He rubbed his fingers as the image of the parlor with the mysterious mirror over the fireplace popped into his head. He raised his eyes toward Stephanie.

"Don't cancel, Stephanie. I'm going to stay there this weekend after all."

CHAPTER 8

"Restless Time"

Kirby began the task of putting his life back to order. After ignoring persistent phone calls from Liana at all hours, he'd received so many angry text messages in rapid succession that he finally blocked her phone number. He cleaned his apartment, boxing Liana's belongings to take to her when things simmered down.

His parents called him from Auckland. They were on a three-week cruise to Australia and New Zealand, and had just returned from a land excursion, so they were checking in before they boarded their ship.

After exchanging greetings with his dad and asking about the trip, Kirby described the package of genealogy information he'd received from Marion and the possible connections to Étienne and Clothiste.

"Étienne and Clothiste. A French soldier from the American Revolution, huh?" His father Patrick's voice faded as he turned from the phone and said something to his wife. "Let me put you on speaker phone so your mom can hear this. She always wanted to have ancestors who served back then."

"Hey, Kirby. How's my baby boy? So, is it true? We have

ancestors from the Revolutionary War?" Rachel Lawrence's cheerful voice brought a smile to her son's face. Kirby repeated the news he had just shared with his dad.

"Uncle Marion's research revealed that one of the Lawrence ancestors married and went to Ireland. His family lived there for a couple of generations. Their children had French names. At least the set of twins did," Kirby finished.

"How exciting!" Rachel's excitement dwindled as she added, "Darn, I forgot that's the Lawrence side of the family in those documents, not mine. Oh, well, I'll have to live vicariously through your father's heritage. But before you tell me more, what's the matter? You don't sound quite like yourself. What's up?"

He should have known his mother would detect something was wrong. She always seemed to know. He explained about the breakup, leaving out the details of the up-close and personal encounter with Liana and her lover Spencer. His parents had accepted Liana as his fiancée, but he had always suspected they were never enamored of her.

"Sorry to hear that, son," his dad said from the background.

Rachel Lawrence echoed the sentiment. "Aw, baby, sorry to hear that news. How are you doing?"

"I'm actually doing okay, Mom. It's been coming for a while. I guess I just ignored all the signs."

"Well, you're on leave. Couldn't you fly out to Australia and meet us after the cruise? We're spending an extra week in Sydney. It would be great, we could spend Thanksgiving together down under."

"Man, it's tempting, Mom. I've always wanted to see Australia. But I've got interviews with a couple of civilian orthopedic practices next week, so neither the jet lag nor the tickets would be worth it for the short time I could travel. Remember, I'm only on leave for a few more weeks. I've got to make up my mind by the end of the year whether I will retire or not."

"But you'll be all alone at Thanksgiving. We could cancel

our stay in Sydney."

"No, don't do that. I'll be fine. It's not like I had any real plans. Even if I was still with Liana, she doesn't cook, let alone bake a turkey. We always just went out somewhere if I was home for the holiday. But I can always go to the hospital and have dinner with the duty team. Don't worry about me. You guys have fun."

After chatting for a few more minutes, Kirby said goodbye to his parents and hung up.

Seconds later, his phone rang again. This time it was Stephanie Kincaid.

"Hello, Kirby, how are you?"

"Fine, Stephanie. What can I do for you?"

"Well, I'm afraid I'm calling to tell you I have to cancel your stay at Clothiste's Inn after all. We discovered some damage this morning and have to close the inn for repairs."

"What happened?"

Stephanie sighed. "Terry and Mary Jo have suffered so many setbacks to opening this place. This time, apparently, someone in the cleaning crew shoved a vacuum cleaner too close to the upstairs water heater and broke the faucet. Water dripped all night and broke through the ceiling. Mary Jo's boyfriend Chase is over there now starting the repairs, but it'll be a while before we can open for guests."

"Wow, tough break. I was really looking forward to staying there." Kirby now wished he had arranged to go back sooner. He had really wanted to check out the mirror over the fireplace again. His face brightened as an idea struck him.

"Hey, Stephanie, will the Inn be re-opened by Thanksgiving? My folks are out of the country and I think I'd like to stay there for the holiday. If you're open."

"Oh, let me check. Hold on a minute." Stephanie muffled the speaker as she spoke to someone. A moment later the clarity to her voice returned and she said, "Terry says she will open for you that weekend on one condition."

"Which is?"

"You have to come to Thanksgiving at her parents' house."

47

Protests sputtered from Kirby's mouth, and Stephanie interrupted. "Forget about arguing, because you won't win with this family. So just say yes and I'll arrange for both."

"Uh...okay. If you think it's..."

"Trust me, it's fine. And Kyle and I are making some progress with your possible connections to the family. If any significant news comes up, I'll let you know beforehand. We planned to update everyone on our research projects at the dinner, so we can include yours at the same time. What do you think?" Her voice dropped to a conspiratorial whisper. "And even if you say no, we'll have the inn open. But I hope you'll come. You're practically family, you know."

Kirby pondered. On the one hand, he had no plans, now that he and Liana had broken up. On the other, wouldn't he feel awkward joining the big, boisterous clan on a family holiday?

You're practically family, you know. Stephanie's words echoed.

"You win, Stephanie. I'll be there. But if you find out anything significant about my family tree, don't make me wait until Thanksgiving to learn about it."

"Deal. We'll start gathering about eleven. Dinner is at three. Are you ready to write down the address?"

Kirby tapped his pockets and came up empty. "No, hold on, I have to find a pen."

"How about I just text it to you?"

"All right, thanks, Stephanie. I appreciate the invitation and tell Terry and Mary Jo I am sorry about the water leak."

He and Stephanie exchanged goodbyes and hung up. A moment later, his incoming text signal pinged and he received the address for the Dunbar home.

***

Thanksgiving Day dawned crisp and cold. The GPS instructed Kirby to turn left, and he entered what he thought was a rural secondary road. As he rounded a bend and cleared the row of trees, the Dunbar antebellum home came into view and Kirby realized the quarter-mile stretch was actually the driveway. He gave a low whistle through clenched teeth as he parked near a row of other vehicles.

Large columns with hanging baskets of fall mums graced a covered front porch that wrapped around both sides of the house. He guessed it probably extended around the back as well, giving the family a splendid view of the Nansemond River peeking over the rises in the land. Six wooden rocking chairs lined the front. Five chairs bearing autumn-colored cushions rocked in time with occasional gusts of wind, while in the sixth a scarecrow sat in a whimsical pose. Smoke curled from one of two chimneys on either side. of the house.

Kirby got out of his car, one hand grabbing the box with four bottles of wine, and the other hefting a Thanksgiving-themed floral arrangement. He swept his gaze over the two-story brick house, with several dormer windows jutting from the roof. On the lawn to his left, a brightly-colored scarecrow stood guard over dozens of pumpkins scattered over bales of hay.

One hundred feet from the main house, a two-story double-car garage sat at a right angle. Stairs along the side led up to a small balcony, where Terry appeared on the landing, carrying a pot wrapped in a quilted cover. As she started down the stairs, her boyfriend Kyle followed, shutting the door adorned in fall decorations. He carried a shopping bag and the couple reached the bottom steps as Kirby approached the apartment.

"Happy Thanksgiving, Kirby," Terry called. "We're so glad you accepted the invitation."

"Thanks for having me. I guess the handshakes will have to wait until we have empty hands." Kirby laughed as he fell in step with the other two.

"Just be ready for the onslaught when you get inside. First, be aware of Mom's number one rule—no handshakes, only hugs. Kids and dogs will be underfoot, a rather cantankerous Hannah will control the kitchen, and Dad and my brothers will be hunkered around a tiny television screen outside waiting for

49

the games to start, while Dad deep-fries a turkey."

Kyle said, "Hopefully, Stephanie and I can fill you in on where you fit in with the family."

Kirby stopped short, as if he'd run into a brick wall. "You found something?"

Kyle nodded. "Put the pieces together just last night."

The trio stepped onto the huge front porch at the same time that a pickup truck rolled down the driveway and parked near the house. Mary Jo and Chase got out of the vehicle, waved, and began unloading trays from the back. Another vehicle pulled up behind the truck, and a man and woman Kirby had never seen before exited.

"Be prepared for the ruckus when you enter," Kyle warned the newcomers with a laugh. "I'll give you the short version of the story in a minute, and the rest of the details after dinner."

Before he could say anything further, the front door burst open. Tanner and Norrie dashed onto the porch, followed by two copper Irish setters. Whoops and hollers from the kids sent the dogs into a barking frenzy as all four bounded from the steps and circled the three adults. When the four occupants of the pickup reached the steps, the dogs barked friendly greetings and scampered down the sidewalk to greet the other groups of arrivals.

Caught up in the flow of kids, dogs, and family members, Kirby and Kyle were separated. Kirby was ushered into the foyer and towards the space comprising a great room open to a huge gourmet kitchen. The tantalizing scents of turkey and sage, apples and cinnamon, fresh bread, and pumpkin pie spices permeated the air. Hannah appeared from nowhere and took the flowers and carton of wine from his arms. She winked at Kirby.

Joan Dunbar, the matriarch of the family, made her way through the family throng and stopped before him with a warm hug of greeting.

"Thanks for having me for dinner, Mrs. Dunbar." Per Terry's counsel, Kirby folded his arms around the woman in a bear hug. She wore the same perfume as his mother, and the pang of regret overcoming him because his parents were not with him was quickly assuaged by Joan's comforting welcome.

"We're all on a first name basis here, Kirby. And you're family. Look." She pointed over her shoulder and Kirby's gaze followed in the same direction.

He first noticed that the furniture had been pushed against the walls to make room for an L-shaped array of banquet tables extending from the kitchen counter area into the family room. Small dishes of autumn flowers nestled amongst unlit orange and green tapers in pumpkin holders.

Finally, his gaze landed on Joan's target and his eyes widened at the huge banner strung across the festive fireplace mantle. He mouthed the words printed in colorful letters as Joan proclaimed the words out loud, "Welcome to the family, Kirby!"

CHAPTER 9

"For the Good Times"

After a round of boisterous greetings with the family, Kirby was shuffled to the backyard, where he spent the next half hour with Charles Dunbar and the other men. Under a pop-up canopy, they huddled around an outdoor deep-fryer. A turkey bubbled in oil as a supplement to the turkey and ham roasting in the kitchen.

Correction. Charles ruled the fryer while his sons and Chase drank hot coffee and offered cooking advice which he ignored. Frosty wisps of air nipped exposed faces and hands as the men bantered back and forth, munching from a tray laden with chicken wings, vegetable strips, and pigs in a blanket. An electronic tablet propped on a small table kept the men up to date on the footballs games. Brothers Gage and Connor supported opposing pro teams, while Charles and Chase followed the college games.

A retired naval physician, Charles ignored the games to engage Kirby in a lively discussion of the many similarities and vast differences each man had experienced as doctors in the Navy.

Clouds darkened overhead as a mist of snow crystals

swirled outside the canopy. Wind sent flakes under the canvas. Sizzling hisses followed the tap of each icy pellet dancing onto the hot fryer's metal surface.

Chase wiped a few specks from the tablet's screen and said, "I'm not sure the weatherman got the forecast right tonight. Looks like that ten percent chance of flurries has drastically increased along with the Cowboys' chances of losing the game."

"Oh, now you're rooting for Dallas." Gage winged an empty paper cup toward Chase, who caught it with a deft wrist maneuver.

"And you still throw like a girl," Chase shot back.

Kirby enjoyed the camaraderie, reminding him of the banter he shared with his hospital colleagues. Cold air seeped through his trousers, shooting sporadic but painful reminders of the titanium and stainless-steel implants that replaced bones in his body. The ache intensified, and he shifted to ease the discomfort.

"Hey, Kirby, you're closest to the door," Charles called. "Will you ask Joan to give you the platter for this bird? It's about ready to come out of the fryer."

"Sure." Kirby turned and ambled to the French doors that lead to the family room. He shivered and hunched in his coat as a few snowflakes slithered down his collar.

The aromas again tantalized Kirby's taste buds as he stepped back into the warm house. The dogs broke into raucous yelps, but instead of charging his way as he expected, they scampered to the foyer. The front door opened, and Sandi entered, grocery bags in both arms. She dropped the bags, shooing the dogs away as she shrugged from her coat and hung it in the closet.

A new wave of commotion began as she brought the parcels to the kitchen. The kids scattered coloring books and crayons in their hasty scramble from the floor. Sandi deposited the bags on the counter, then bent to hug the kids, who wrapped their arms around her hips.

"It's snowing, guys," she said. Squeals of delight followed, and the kids leapt into frantic jumping jacks, tiny arms spinning like windmills. They raced to look out of the bay window at the back of the kitchen, kneeling on chairs to wipe frost from the windows and peer out.

Sandi smiled and began working her way around the room to greet family members. She wore her dark hair swept up in a stylish bun. Cold air had left rosy red marks on her cheeks, emphasizing her green eyes. Her sweater, a deeper green, which Kirby thought probably had some trendy name like emerald or jade, clung to her curves.

The tasty Thanksgiving aromas disappeared from Kirby's mind as his gaze settled on the far more delectable sight of the pretty lawyer. He had long forgotten his mission to retrieve the turkey platter.

Stephanie slipped beside him and offered him a welcoming cup of coffee. "How did the bonding with the Dunbar men go?" she asked.

"Wh-what?" Kirby stuttered, tearing his gaze to meet Stephanie's amused brown eyes, her dimple deepening in her smile as she pushed the steaming mug toward him. She held a wine glass in her other hand. Kirby took the coffee and stumbled on, "They're all great guys. How'd you do with the Dunbar gals?"

"Oh, I've been banished from the kitchen. I can't cook very well, and once I finished my relegated duties of slicing and dicing, I just got in their way. I'm serving on clean-up detail anyway. Terry's about as lame in the kitchen as I am, but I suspect she's trying to bribe someone to take over her share of the clean-up. She's desperate enough to pay the kids. Look," Stephanie said with a laugh, "I think she's cornered Sandi in the dining room and offered her Maserati in payment if Sandi will join the cleanup committee."

Kirby couldn't prevent his eyes from darting toward the dining room. From his angle he couldn't see her, but his heart skipped at Sandi's name.

Trying to appear casual, he asked, "Can you clear things up for me, tell me again who is who and how they are related to the family? I know some of the connections, but I've lost track of names. There are some new faces here that I don't recognize." Kirby scratched his head as he looked around the open rooms bustling with family members.

Stephanie smiled, dimpling again. "Overwhelming, isn't it? I was an only child and when I came to the first family event, I was scared to death to be around so many people at once." She drew Kirby out of the path of the chaos and closer to the fireplace. "Okay, you know the Dunbar parents are Charles and Joan. Their elder son Gage is my firefighting fiancé, whom I met this summer when my ancestry research brought me to Portsmouth. His younger brother, Connor, and Beth are Tanner's parents. They are expecting baby number two."

Stephanie laughed and pointed as Conner helped Beth rise from an awkward position on the floor where she had been coloring with Tanner and Norrie. Stephanie turned her hand toward the kitchen where Hannah withdrew a golden turkey from the oven.

"Mmm." Both Kirby and Stephanie hummed with appreciation as the aroma seemed to float on the heat waves rising from the oven. Stephanie continued, "Joan and Hannah are distant cousins but grew up together. Hannah was gone for several years and when she developed cancer, Joan took her in until she recovered. Hannah returned the favor by acting as a nanny when Joan returned to her job as a professor."

"Does she always wear those snarky tee-shirts?" Kirby asked. Hannah's autumn-orange shirt choice, worn over brown tights, matched the holiday decorations. Today's shirt featured a picture of a turkey roasting behind a glass oven door, and the caption underneath proclaimed, "You're really looking in a mirror." Instead of her customary colorful Crocs, she wore ankle-high brown boots.

"You know, I don't know that I have ever seen her dressed in anything but her crazy shirts. It will make buying Christmas presents a breeze. By the way, have you noticed that there is not a sign of green and red around here? Some people put their Christmas decorations up mid-November, but Joan and

Charles refuse to display any signs of Christmas until the day after Thanksgiving. However, Charles is ready to go all out tomorrow."

"That's how it should be," Kirby agreed. "I make it home about every two years for the holidays. My folks visit in the alternate years, except this year they are on a cruise to Australia and New Zealand until the first week of December. I miss them."

"Oh, I've always wanted to go to Australia," Stephanie proclaimed. Following a pop, laughter burst from the kitchen and they glanced in that direction. Mary Jo held a bottle of champagne and the family surrounding her tipped heads upwards. Joan pointed to the champagne cork caught up in the chandelier.

Stephanie smiled. "It's good to see Mary Jo so relaxed and happy. When I first met her, she had just gotten out of the Army and was going through a rough time in her life. She's been Terry's best friend since grade school, and when she was about twelve her home life became very difficult. The Dunbars applied for guardianship, and Mary Jo lived with them as a foster child."

"They're an amazing family," Kirby said. He sipped from his coffee cup, gazing over the rim at the warm scene in the kitchen.

"That's not the half of it. Mary Jo's fiancé was friends of the family too. When Chase was a teenager, his mother remarried. The step-father became abusive to both Chase and his mother, and Chase started getting into trouble. He and Gage got into some heavy-duty mischief with another boy, vandalizing a lot of property. The other boy got away with his part, but Charles made the other two delinquents work the entire summer to repair and pay for the damage. Under Charles' stern tutelage, Chase discovered a talent for building things. Joan recognized the signs of abuse and helped his mother get away from the relationship. He adores them and credits them with saving his life. Then in high school, he and Mary Jo were a thing until they had a major falling out and she joined the Army just like that." Stephanie snapped her fingers. "They didn't see each other for ten years, but they found each other again. And there's more to their story. Let me refill my wine glass. Would you like any?"

Kirby shook his head and waited by the fireplace until Stephanie returned. He had gotten used to the din around him, but the crackling of the fire offered comfort as well as warmth.

"Okay, so to continue. No one in the family ever knew that Hannah had given up a son for adoption." She waved her pinky toward a tall man standing between Mary Jo and another woman. "That's her son, Wayne. After he retired, he began researching his family tree, and he contacted Kyle because of some common names they both shared in an online tree."

"Wow, that's the stuff soap operas are made of."

"Every family has such a story." Stephanie nodded. "I found out I was adopted. Then Kyle and I connected during my family tree research. Now he and Terry are engaged. In fact, we have joked that he is our common denominator. Kyle has been the link for each of us to learn who we all are and where we came from. And pretty soon, you're going to find out how you, as a descendant of Louis, fit in with the rest of us."

"I've felt some kind of connection from the moment I saw the inn. Just something about it drew me in, like it called to me."

"Me too. You know, it's haun…"

The back door opened and Gage poked his head around the edge, snowflakes glistening on his hair. A blast of frigid air caused the flames in the fireplace to leap into a dance. He caught sight of Kirby. "Hey, man, where's the turkey platter?" He slid his hand along the wall and flipped a light switch. The outdoor area behind him flooded with light.

"Oh, damn, I forgot." Kirby looked in confusion from the back door to the kitchen.

"I've got it, Gage," Sandi called from across the room. Gage nodded and shut the door. She picked up a ceramic plate and smiled at Kirby as she walked toward them. His gaze locked with hers, and once again his heart thumped. A dose of pure lust coursed through him.

He didn't know the woman, but he knew he fell in love with her at that moment.

"She's not married," Stephanie whispered. Kirby opened his mouth to protest but she dragged him toward the approaching woman.

Now would be a good time for his bad leg to act up and prevent him from moving. But the leg cooperated, and Kirby was thrust further toward the object of his admiration.

***

In spite of the cold air that rushed in when Gage poked his head around the door and called for the turkey platter, warmth pooled under Sandi's turtleneck as her gaze caught Kirby's. For days now, the doctor's face had seemed to fill her every waking thought despite her efforts to shake him away. Even though Stephanie had mentioned that he had broken up with his fiancée, she'd tamped down the flutter of interest. She had neither time nor inclination for romantic notions.

But in her mind, his image appeared over and over.

She gripped the huge platter with both hands and stepped around the counter, heading straight toward the French doors beside the fireplace where the handsome doctor stood.

All she could manage to do was nod and say, "Nice to see you, Kirby."

"Same here, Sandi." He opened the door and she stepped out onto the porch.

The exact same thought crossed each of their minds at the exact same time.

Geez, you couldn't think of anything better to say?

CHAPTER 10

"Time of the Season"

"How big is the snow out there now, Tanner?" Norrie clambered on the seat of a small wooden bench and knelt beside Tanner. The kids formed blinders with their hands and pressed their foreheads to the glass to peer into the dusk. Small circles of mist formed each time they exhaled.

"Here comes Daddy now. Let's ask him." Tanner shouted. Foot stomps thumped outside, the French door opened, and Connor Dunbar bustled in with an armful of firewood. Gage followed, arms also loaded.

Tanner rushed to his father. "How big is the snow, Daddy? Can we go out and make a snowman?"

Connor stacked the firewood and turned to Tanner, holding his thumb and forefinger about a half-inch apart. "It's this big now, but I don't think your moms are going to let you out tonight. Maybe tomorrow."

Beth walked over and held a hand out to each of the kids. "We'll worry about making snowmen tomorrow, okay, kids? Right now, Grampie and Chase are going to have their turkey-carving contest, then we'll go wash for dinner." She stopped near the counter to let the children admire the feast before the carving began. The rest of the family lined up behind the kids. Kirby stood behind Norrie, Sandi to his left. She shifted. He inhaled a whiff of her perfume before the next waft of food overwhelmed the delicate scent.

When Connor hefted Tanner to his shoulders for a better view, Norrie turned around. Instead of going to her mother's outstretched arms, the little girl lifted her arms to Kirby, who obliged and picked her up.

"Thank you," Sandi said with a smile.

"No problem," Kirby responded. Norrie settled in his right arm, her small hands curled around his neck. As he steadied his stance, his left shoulder touched Sandi's, body warmth radiating through their sweaters.

Sandi stiffened and Kirby expected her to move away, but Stephanie's close proximity on the other side allowed little room to maneuver.

"What are they doing, Mommy?" Norrie asked.

"Chase and Mr. Charles are going to have a contest to see who does the fastest job of carving the turkeys, sweetie."

Beside the golden oven-roasted bird and its deep-fried relative, a ham studded with cloves glistened under a glazed topping. Platters of food covered the countertop.

Chase stood poised with an electric carving knife and fork hovering over the oven-baked turkey. Charles picked up a traditional knife and posed over his prospective work of art. The two men glared at each other, but their twinkling eyes revealed it was all in fun.

"Hold that pose," Hannah ordered, hoisting a camera hanging from her neck. She snapped several photos and let the camera dangle from the cord. She held up a napkin and added, "On your mark."

"It's showtime," Charles said with a snarl. He flicked his wrist, twisting the knife around.

"Get set." Hannah raised the napkins higher and Joan twisted the cylinders of a small timer.

"You're on, old man," Chase responded, a sneer curling one side of his lip. He pushed the electric on-off switch twice, emitting twin "whir-whir" sounds.

"Go!" Hannah dropped the napkin and Joan clicked the start button on the timer. The family broke into cheers as the two men began the task of carving the birds.

While Chase had the advantage of the electric knife, Charles displayed the confidence that years of practice—and a razor-sharp titanium-bladed knife—brought. The two men sawed their way, slabs of meat piling at almost equal increments.

"Grampie's gonna win!" Tanner shouted, rocking on his dad's shoulders.

Chase growled and made zapping motions with the knife in Tanner's direction, sending the kids into peals of laughter. The action stole a precious split second that enabled Charles' manual cutting to catch up.

"DING!" The timer pinged at the minute mark. Both men set their knives down and stepped from the counter with their palms out.

Due to his newcomer status, Mary Jo's father was deemed to be the least biased person in the room. Joan handed him a six-inch ruler. Wayne made a good-natured production of measuring each stack, and then measuring again. Much to the kids' delight, he spoke in a perfect imitation of Yoda and said, "Hmm, higher this one is," and pointed to Charles' platter.

The family erupted into cheers and applause.

"Rookie." Charles raised his hands overhead in a victory clasp and smirked at Chase.

Tanner shouted, "I knew you'd win, Grampie."

"Rematch—here—Christmas," Chase said, pointing at the counter. He and Charles broke into laughter, shook hands and man-hugged.

"Okay, everybody, let's get ready for dinner," Hannah rasped. Kirby and Connor set the kids on the floor. Beth stepped up to take the children to wash up for dinner.

Like a well-oiled machine, the various family members sprang into action. Chase opened a bottle of wine to breathe. Charles sliced ham. The Dunbar brothers got glasses and filled ice buckets. Stephanie lit candles while the other women placed covered dishes in metal stands on the table.

"What can I do?" Kirby and Kyle asked in unison.

"Just relax," Joan and Hannah said at the same time. "Have a glass of wine," Joan added, as she set baskets of rolls on the tables.

"I think I'd just be in the way, anyway," Kyle said as he walked to the counter where Chase had set the wine. He poured a glass and handed it to Kirby. He poured another. Picking it up, he raised it to the welcome banner.

"We haven't had the chance to talk," Kyle said. "Joan likes to have what she calls family summits to bring everyone up-to-date on family news, so I'll be explaining everything to the whole crowd all at once after dinner. But in a nutshell, you are a direct descendant of Étienne and Clothiste Rocher, descended from a long line of sons all the way back to their son Louis."

"How can that be if Lawrence has been my family's name for generations?"

Kyle smiled. "You do come from a long line of Lawrence sons. When daughters are involved, the changes from maiden to married name can blur records and make things a bit harder to track, but with sons, it can be much easier. However, in some cases, like with your family, there are different issues because sometimes French names, although unique, give researchers a lot of headaches due to variations, misspellings, and the names chosen by sons to differentiate from their fathers."

"Genealogy later," Terry interrupted, and kissed Kyle's cheek. "Dinner is on." She slipped her hands through the crooks of each man's arm and steered them toward the table, where Charles stood at one end, Joan to his left.

"Terry, you and Kyle sit there," Stephanie said, indicating two chairs on one side of the table. "And, Kirby, you are over here."

She touched the back of a chair to Charles' right. Kirby pulled out the designated chair but remained standing. Like a stage director, Stephanie guided Mary Jo's father Wayne to the opposite end of the table, with Hannah on his right and Elizabeth on his left.

Both sides of the table filled up. The kids scooted into their side-by-side chairs, extra cushions providing additional height. Beth and Connor filled out the rest of the table. After settling Norrie in the seat, Sandi stepped to Kirby's right.

Terry and Kyle were joined on their side of the table by Stephanie and Gage, Mary Jo and Chase. Kirby caught the satisfied smile in Stephanie's face as she glanced around the table. He suspected she had engineered the layout to ensure he sat next to Sandi. He cast his eyes to his right and studied Sandi's profile.

He could think of a lot worse places to be than beside this beautiful woman.

Tanner raised his hand and called, "Grammie, can I say the grace today?"

"Well, of course." Joan smiled. She bowed her head, and the family followed suit.

Tanner tented his hands and bowed his head, reciting the traditional Catholic blessing perfectly. With a wink at his grandson, Charles added, "Bless the family gathered here and the friends who are as dear as family. We look forward to the future arrival of another Dunbar grandchild, and welcome Kirby as a newly-discovered member of the family. We also thank you for bringing Wayne to Hannah and Mary Jo. May we enjoy Your bountiful blessings today and pray for everyone's safe passage home."

Choruses of "Amen!" followed. Conversation flowed as the clink of dishes and silverware signaled the start of the bountiful feast.

Any reservations Kirby may have had about spending Thanksgiving in the home of relative strangers disappeared in the family's warm welcome. Despite multiple conversations going on at once, the atmosphere was one of good-natured teasing and light-hearted conversation. The family was so relaxed and welcoming that he felt as if he had known them his entire life. The feeling seemed mutual.

All the while, Kirby remained physically aware of Sandi's proximity, catching occasional whiffs of her perfume whenever she turned in his direction. She was left-handed, and with chairs crowded rather close, they often bumped elbows.

They often bumped knees as well. She sat to the right of his bad leg and shifted frequently to help Norrie. Every now and then her leg brushed his. Sometimes she jiggled her leg in a jittery dance before settling. The calm only lasted a few seconds before she began fidgeting again. Kirby found the nervous habit endearing and sensual at the same time. While his instinct reminded him he had a scarred, disfigured leg and encouraged a distance between them, his inner soul enjoyed the physical contact.

"Mom, you told us Kirby is another descendant of Étienne and Clothiste. When are you going to explain how he fits into this family?" Gage asked as he reached for a casserole dish and spooned candied yams onto his plate. Before Joan could answer, he added, "And, Kirby, I hope you are ready for ghosts and ghouls and things that go bump in the night."

Joan turned and smiled at Kirby, resting her hand on his forearm. "I hope you don't mind waiting a little longer for all the answers, Kirby. Kyle and Stephanie have drawn up a chart to show us after dinner that will give us all the details. They've done a tremendous job piecing together some interesting stories to tell us and it's so much easier to understand while looking at the family tree."

Kirby nodded. "So then, tell me about those ghosts and ghouls and things that go bump in the night."

Joan nodded and took a sip of iced tea before speaking. "Like several of the other historic houses in Olde Towne, the three buildings, especially what is now the B and B, have been called haunted. All three houses were once owned by the family. My Aunt Ida lived in one house her whole life and when she died, she left it to Terry. It's the house where Terry's law office is. For the other two houses, ownership changed hands several times for the homes where the inn and café are before they were bought back into the family. Over the years, people have claimed to see images of young girls, and other figures have manifested in and around the buildings. Family lore reports that people have heard laughter, crying, and other noises."

"For the record, I don't believe in ghosts, Joan." Kirby smiled. "But Stephanie has already tried to convince me that some family members set off sparks when they touch. I'll admit I have noticed several occurrences, especially when I first met you, but my technical mind can only accept it as static electricity or something scientific."

With a laugh, Joan said, "Charles says the same thing, as these unusual events rarely happen around him. Up until Stephanie arrived, it had been years since anyone reported seeing any strange phenomena. Then the ghosts of the three little colonial sisters began to appear again, as well as the evil spirit. Since the skeleton was reburied, we haven't had any more sightings. I understand you're spending the weekend at Clothiste's Inn. Are you looking for ghosts, Kirby Lawrence?"

Kirby shook his head. "Like I said, I don't believe in ghosts. But I'll admit something has drawn me to the inn. *If* I'm family and *if* there are ghosts, maybe I will see one when I spend the night there." Kirby drizzled a little gravy onto his plate and dabbed the remaining piece of turkey in it.

"Well, I can say for sure you are part of our family, Kirby. As for the ghosts…" Joan smiled, lifted her hands palms up, and shrugged. "Let's enjoy our meal and talk more later."

CHAPTER 11

"Time Waits for No One""

Dessert plates replaced dinner plates as many hands made light work of clearing the tables. Kirby offered to help, but he, Sandi, and a tired, pregnant Beth were ordered to sit back and relax. Stephanie moved food from platters to smaller dishes, Connor and Gage loaded the dishwasher, Hannah and Terry brought pies and cakes to the table. Charles made coffee while Joan set cups and saucers at the adult seats. Terry placed mugs of hot chocolate in front of the kids.

"Mommy, can I rest my head on your lap while my chocolate cools?" Norrie asked as she yawned.

"Sure." Sandi scooted her chair back, moving a bit closer to Kirby to make room for Norrie to lower her head. She rubbed her daughter's forehead in slow, short circles.

"When my mom did that to me when I was a kid, I was asleep in a flash," Kirby said. "Norrie is an unusual name. Is she named after someone in your family?"

Sandi shifted, her shoulder brushing against Kirby. He didn't move away, and they remained like that for several seconds before she answered. "It's a combination of my mom's first and middle names, Norah Leigh. So, I just used part of each name and came up with Norrie."

"That's cute." Kirby enjoyed the comfortable warmth of body heat as he and Sandi sat close, shoulders pressed together. Tanner called for Norrie to come watch *Despicable Me 2* on a DVD. Norrie scrambled to a sitting position and bumped her head on the table, rattling dishes. Sandi scooted her chair back and helped her daughter to the area where Tanner waited.

Kirby had a perfect view of Sandi's shapely butt as she bent to angle the girl's chair towards the DVD player on the table. Although their bodies no longer touched, Kirby hardened when thoughts of a naked Sandi lying beneath him flashed into his mind. He shifted with embarrassment and concentrated on the flipchart Kyle stood beside.

Kyle cleared his throat. "We've all welcomed Kirby into the family. Until tonight, he thought he came from a long line of Irish and English, which he does, along with one Italian grandmother. But we were able to dig a little further than what he knew, and we established his French connection to the colonial family." The lanky professor's voice took on a lecturer's tone. "Once I started working on the brother Louis' family tree, it was evident this would be one of the easiest ancestry lines I've ever documented. Through the wonders of the internet, and the meticulous records kept by the various generations who followed Étienne and Clothiste, Stephanie and I located unequivocal proof that Kirby is indeed a descendant of their son Louis."

The kids burst into lively giggles at some mischief the Minions were up to and everyone glanced toward their table with smiles.

Kyle tapped the chart with an old pointer left over from Joan's days as a college professor. "As I mentioned to Kirby a little while ago, he comes from an unbroken line of Lawrence males, so that made it a little easier to verify the lineage than it might have been if there had been a daughter along the way."

"If all the males in my Lawrence line descended from Étienne, how did our family name change from Rocher?"

Kirby asked. He forgot about his pumpkin pie as he leaned in to listen closely.

"This is something that happened frequently in French, French-Canadian and particularly Acadian families. Since Louis was born in French Canada, in Acadia, Nova Scotia to be exact, it appears he adopted the custom of many men to differentiate from their fathers or siblings. Many added a '*dit*' name. The French word '*dit*' translated to English means 'called.' This second surname was used as an additional way to identify the family line. Not every French family in France or in French Canada adopted this practice, but it happened often enough that it can stymie a family researcher. Add spelling variations, duplicate families with the same names, and conversions of names to their English sound, it can become a genealogical nightmare."

"Excuse me while I put on more coffee." Joan rose from the table and on the way to the kitchen area stopped at the chart. She pointed to Etienne's name on the chart and swept her finger to the one above it.

"Even Étienne's father has a variation of names, which we learned when Stephanie translated some of the family records written in French. Phillipe de la Rocher's second wife Abigail, who was English, persuaded him to anglicize his name to Phillip Rocker, which proved to be a great asset in his business dealings when he immigrated to America."

"That's correct," Kyle nodded. "Then, his son Étienne met Clothiste several years after he arrived in Canada with the French Army. They married and stayed in Acadia after the war with Britain. Like many Acadians, their family was eventually expelled by the British. They lost everything and moved into northern New York near the St. Lawrence River. They retained the family name de la Rocher, which was the maiden name of all of the daughters on their marriage licenses."

Kirby understood that Kyle was setting the stage for the announcement as explanation rather than suspense, but the anticipation *was* killing him. He bounced his right leg on the ball of his foot, bumping Sandi's leg. She slipped her hand on his knee and gave a reassuring pat before removing it.

"I'm sorry," Sandi whispered, a blush creeping around her neck. "That was an automatic reaction. You might have noticed that I sometimes do the identical thing. Norrie and I both have the same habit, and we pat each other's knees to remind ourselves to stop."

The fleeting touch had done more than stop Kirby's restless leg. It had stirred his restless heart—and broken his concentration as it stirred another part of his body.

"I'm sorry, Kyle, I missed what you said," he said.

Sandi giggled under her breath and Kirby tapped her elbow with his. They exchanged smiles.

"So, we know that Louis was born in Acadia but spent much of his early years in the town near the St. Lawrence River, before they moved into the New England states when Etienne joined the French forces fighting for America. As a young boy Louis took the surname 'dit St. Lawrence' but we suspect when he was groomed to become a spy, he adapted the name to Louis Lawrence to sound more English. I would assume his name was pronounced with the anglicized version rather than the French."

Stephanie interjected. "We know there is an anecdote in one of Clothiste's journals that when Louis was a young boy, he got separated from his family when they left in advance of invading British forces. This set several of the men off on a frantic search. Clothiste was sick with worry but Louis was found safe and sound in the British camp and returned to his family. She wrote that they had behaved kindly toward her child, and he'd explained that he told the soldiers his name was Louis Lawrence, so they would not realize he was a French-Canadian boy, or somehow connect him to the French army."

Kyle nodded. "Right. With a little more research, we determined that a Louis Lawrence, son of a couple listed only as Étienne and Clothiste, married a woman named Elizabeth "Lizzie" Wheeler." He pointed to a name on the tree. "Lizzie came to America from England as an indentured servant to her Aunt Abigail, Phillip's wife. Abigail was a loyalist and became an unwitting pawn in the Portsmouth-based espionage ring involving Louis, his father Étienne, and his grandfather Phillip. Abigail often held dinners for British officials, and as a maid in the household who held nothing but contempt for her aunt, Lizzie picked up information in conversations and delivered it to the spies. She and Louis fell in love and after the war they married. They had a son named Phillip after Etienne's father. Phillip married an Irish woman named Sadie O'Connell. They went to Ireland and had a son, Lewis, spelled L-E-W-I-S, and twins Étienne and Clothiste. That pretty much cemented the lineage of Kirby's family tree and proved he was descended from Étienne and Clothiste de la Rocher."

The family erupted into applause. Joan set the coffee pot on the table and raised her wineglass. She said, "To Clothiste and Etienne…" but choked up. Charles stood and tapped his wineglass. All eyes turned toward the patriarch of the Dunbar family. He held Joan's hand with his left and raised his glass toward Kirby.

"On behalf of Joan and all the descendants of Clothiste and Étienne, I toast these ancestors. May good health and prosperity sustain their descendants for years to come. And, Kirby, let me be the first to officially welcome you to the family."

"And…" Joan recovered her voice and added, proud eyes on Charles before her gaze circled the table. "And to those of you who chose us to be your family, may love shine through our triumphs and tragedies."

"Here, here." Around the table, extended members of the Dunbar clan raised wineglasses and coffee cups.

Kirby's emerald ring warmed and vibrated against his finger. He glanced down. Twinkles of light illuminated the facets of the rectangular stone.

The quiver stilled, and the ring returned to normal.

***

The tapered candles had dwindled to short stubs, flames

spitting as they fought to stay alive. Stephanie pulled some papers from her pocket, and said, "Before we all leave the table, I just wanted to tell you about something else I found out. This has to do with the three cousins during the Civil War era." She glanced around the table. "For those who don't know, I rented the apartment above Terry's law office when I first arrived in Portsmouth. During Hurricane Abby a shutter broke loose. It banged ferociously against the house and I went upstairs to the attic. There was a sudden..." She glanced at Tanner and Norrie, heads together as they engaged in "kid-talk," and then continued, "There was a sudden manifestation that I believe everyone knows about?"

Everyone except the children nodded.

Terry took up the story. "This spirit, which we came to recognize was Abigail, the step-grandmother to our three sisters and Louis, tried to prevent Stephanie from making the discovery. After our girl fought back the—manifestation—she discovered an old metal box. It was full of assorted loose pages from diaries, as well as a stack of old letters, and an old doll that belonged to her ancestress, Nicole." She reached for a glass of water.

Mary Jo, not usually one to elaborate on the odd happenings in Olde Towne, continued. "These three cousins in the eighteen-sixties, who were each a descendant of Etienne and Clothiste's daughters, spent some time together in Portsmouth. Several lived here during the Civil War. It turned out that the family had hidden valuables when Union soldiers occupied the home for a time. When they retrieved the items later, the metal box was overlooked until Steph found it more than a century later."

"That generation was responsible for preserving many of the family records because the women who applied for membership in the Daughters of the American Revolution had to locate and provide a ton of documentation," Kyle added.

Stephanie nodded. "Most of what I have read and catalogued are just interesting insights into the family life at that time, mostly about marriages, births, baptisms, deaths.

Several letters discuss Theresé's death in eighteen sixty-one, shortly after returning from a visit here. There is one brief mention of the time she visited Portsmouth as an old woman and had hallucinations, shouting that the candlesticks were haunted, and one of the men hid the silverware instead of destroying it as she wanted."

"And that silverware was also recently recovered in the attic over the B and B," Mary Jo interjected.

"Right. So anyway, most of the letters are mundane exchanges between cousins Emily and Celestine. I'm still putting them in chronological order. But there was one sad story I wanted to read to you all." She unfolded the papers, tearing one page. She smiled. "Good thing these are photocopies."

Stephanie read aloud.

April Eighteen Sixty-one
Dearest Emily,

I am happy to hear news of your safe return to New Hampshire without incident. It was wonderful to have you visit with us, and I am so happy that you and Thomas may decide to move down here one day. With all of his brothers in Portsmouth, he would be so much closer to his family. I do understand that you must care for your great-grandmama Theresé at your home, and you will not make a decision until her time comes. You know I love her dearly and do not wish the day to come too soon, but I miss you so.

I hesitate to tell you bad news, but I must. I am sad to report horrible news about Daniel and Lauralee's little daughter. It happened just after you left. We had a lovely afternoon tea in the garden, and then sent the children to play. She was playing near the old magnolia tree and disappeared just as a storm arose. The twins went searching for her but came back without her. We are all still in a state of shock since she disappeared. How could an eight-year-old girl vanish into thin air? One minute she is playing hide and seek and the next minute she is nowhere to be found. All the family has searched high and low, even down to the Elizabeth River every day at the change of the tides, and there is no sign of her anywhere. It has been two days, and we can only fear the worst. The constables continue to investigate, but they suggest that gypsies may have kidnapped her.

Lauralee is nearly mad with grief. They were supposed to go back home this evening, but she refused to leave without her daughter. Daniel feels the same way, of course, but he does have to return to his business as soon as possible. He has implied that he will sedate her to get her in the carriage if necessary for their return home tomorrow, but he hopes desperately that they have some answers today. I hope that he does not act too quickly, for I fear Lauralee will never forgive him for that, or that neither will ever recover from the disappearance of their child. I don't know that I would.

We will no longer allow the children to play in the yard unless an adult is present. Every stranger is regarded with suspicion, and indeed even our neighbors have come under scrutiny.

So, dear cousin, I must end with less than happy news. I pray that I will know something before this letter is posted, but if not, I know you would want to know immediately. Should we hear anything, good or bad, I shall dispatch a letter to you with utmost haste.

All my love, dearest cousin,
Celestine

Conversation merged into a sea of voices throwing questions at Stephanie.

"A child disappeared? Did they find her?"

"Who was she?"

"Who is Lauralee?"

Stephanie held up her hands. "She is married to a Lawrence descendant. I don't know any more about her than that. There are stacks of letters that I have been going through, and many of them are out of order. I have not yet matched up other correspondence between Emily and Celestine that may clear up this new mystery. Kyle and I even searched records in Richmond, where the family lived, to see if there were any references to the incident. But there is more about this sad and strange situation." Stephanie swallowed and slid her gaze to Kirby.

As every curious face at the table turned in his direction,

Kirby nodded and waited for Stephanie to continue.

"Kirby, Daniel is a descendant of your Louis, and therefore he and Lauralee are ancestors of yours through their son Frank Michael Lawrence. We didn't know this relationship when we went to Richmond to search for information on the missing child because we hadn't received your Uncle Marion's paperwork at the time. Even so, there is no mention of a daughter in that packet he sent to you, only of the twin sons, one of whom is your third great-grandfather, I believe. Perhaps the person who wrote the history had no knowledge of the little girl's existence, or quite likely just didn't record it since she was not the direct descendant they were tracing in your line. Maybe she was left out of the account because of her tragic disappearance, I just don't know."

"Have you find out anything else about the missing girl?" Kirby asked.

Stephanie shook her head. "Not yet."

"Oh, what a sad note to end on," Sandi said. She patted Kirby's shoulder. "I'm so sorry."

A grandfather clock chimed nine o'clock. Joan offered the guests a place to stay for the night, adding, "The snow has stopped but roads may still be treacherous."

"We're heading out now, Mom," Connor said, stifling a yawn. "I go on duty at eight a.m." He walked over to the couch. Tanner and Norrie nestled asleep under Minion blankets on opposite ends of the couch.

"Yes, and Kyle and I better go too. We have that long, treacherous walk of one hundred feet to my apartment, you know."

"I'm checking in on a patient I am concerned about tomorrow morning.," Kirby said as he rose, "so I need to leave as well. Thanks for a wonderful dinner, Joan, and for letting me share this holiday as a newfound family member."

He extended his hand to Joan before snatching it back and scooping her into a hug. "Oh, yeah, I know the rules now."

"Fast learner," Joan said with a smile as she embraced him.

Kirby exchanged goodbyes with the rest of the family,

hugging each per the rules, coming to Terry last. He said, "I'm expecting to run into some of those colonial ghosts at Clothiste's Inn tomorrow evening."

Terry laughed and drew Kirby to the counter, where she picked up a bag full of containers. "Mom is sending a care package home with you. As far as the B and B, just don't touch the candlesticks," she warned.

Stephanie and Mary Jo said in unison, "For sure."

"Don't go in if the house is cold," Stephanie added.

"And if you see any slithering gray mist, run like hell." Mary Jo interjected. "But if it smells like fresh baking, that's a good sign and you can go in."

Kirby laughed but the three women remained serious. They had already told him some of the experiences they'd encountered at the inn, and while Kirby didn't doubt some kind of phenomena had occurred, his clinical mind just didn't believe in ghosts.

"Okay, stay away from the candlesticks, don't go in if the house is cold inside, and run like hell if the mist appears. Stay if it smells like fresh baking. Got it."

Terry placed her hand on Kirby's forearm and stared into his eyes. "I'm serious. Theresé appeared to me in the flesh, Kirby, but I've seen her image since I was a kid. Those sisters had unresolved issues from their lives, and once we discovered who was buried under the tree and the three jewels were recovered, there hasn't been an unusual occurrence. We thought the past was over and done with."

Sandi followed them to the door, Norrie tucked in her arms. She said, "The future is what we should look forward to."

***

By noon on Black Friday, a warm spell had erased all traces of snow. Even the small mounds formed by snowplows dissolved into puddles due to the rising temperatures. Kirby headed toward the mall to join the other shoppers on the hunt for Christmas bargains. When he entered the access road, traffic stood still as dozens of vehicles waited to enter the parking areas. Cars occupied every space within his field of vision, stretching to the far points of the lot. Other vehicles drove in steady circles down the rows in search of spaces. If the bustle in stores equaled that of the parking lots, merchants should be dancing all the way to the bank. And he wasn't about to jockey with the hordes of bargain hunters. At the first opportunity, he maneuvered toward the main highway.

He wondered if Liana's cash registers jingled with the holiday sales.

It was the first time he had thought of her in days. When he stopped for a red light, he pulled his phone from his pocket and traced circles on the keypad. The light turned green and he replaced the phone without tapping her number.

He glanced at his watch. Three more hours before he could check in at Clothiste's Inn.

With a last look at the line of cars headed to the mall, he headed toward the hospital, stopping by a donut shop to load up with pastries for the on-duty staff.

After distributing boxes at the nurses' station and exchanging pleasantries, Kirby pushed the door to Room 4-28 and peered into the semi-dark room.

The figure outlined under the covers appeared to be an overweight man, but Kirby knew that was a result of the swelling and the injury to the pelvis. Kirby opened the chart for Seaman Trevor Wilson and read through several entries before slipping it into its holder at the foot of the bed, then walked to the patient's side.

The patient's eyes studied him.

"Are you the one who patched me up and saved my leg, doc?" he asked, gesturing with a weak right hand. A navy-blue sling anchored his left arm to his chest to immobilize the broken clavicle.

"Not just me, Trevor." Kirby smiled as he checked the fixator extending from Trevor's body. "It was the whole team, from the radiologist to the internist, the nurses, surgical techs, the corps staff. How are you feeling today?"

Tears slid from the corners of Trevor's eyes, running along his temples to the pillow. He gulped. "Will I be able to walk again, doc?"

A sharp pain sliced through Kirby's thigh—and his mind. *Sympathy pains?* Had not the same worry entered his mind when he first became aware of his own injuries?

"Trevor, there is nothing to indicate you won't walk again, but I'm not going to lie to you. You have a long, and probably difficult recovery ahead, but you should be able to walk again. We'll get you in rehab as soon as your bones have healed enough."

"But I'm busted up pretty bad, doc, head to foot. I made my mom take a picture and show me. From the back of my shoulders to my heels, I'm nothing but solid black and blue. My left leg is in a cast from my hip to my foot, my left shoulder trussed like a turkey wing. My balls are the size of grapefruits. I thought I was bleeding down there and made my mom check. I saw her face and made her take a picture and show me that too. I'm no good anymore, doc. I couldn't stop my mom from coming, but I told my girl she couldn't come. If I'm so damaged, my girlfriend will leave me." He turned his head away from Kirby. "I wish I'd just died on that ship."

Kirby pushed a stool to the bedside, swiveled the seat to a higher position and sat, elbows leaning on thighs as he studied the floor.

"Trevor, I want you to look at me and listen to what I have to say, understand?" He raised his head and looked into his patient's eyes.

Trevor nodded.

"I'm going to tell you something that happened to me, that only my doctors and my parents know about."

And maybe some things I've never told another living soul.

CHAPTER 12

"Beat the Clock"

Louis
Somewhere in time

Louis clamped his hands over his ears. The incessant clanging of the clock echoed in the room that trapped his soul between heaven and earth. Or perhaps hell and earth.

How long had it been? He had no way of knowing. He'd long ago lost track of whether the clock was tolling day or night. He had roamed this dark space, rarely hearing a sound other than his shuffling feet or the tolling of a faraway clock.

Except for the one time a little boy called his name, providing the first new sound he'd heard since his entrapment.

For those same countless days—or years—he saw only the mysterious light that would appear in the wall and disappear.

Except for that same night when he saw the man holding the little boy, visible in the small square of light.

The man who looks like me. The boy who looks like my son.

Louis paused in his pacing. Only eleven chimes sounded this time. He always counted them, waiting for the twelfth stroke and the scene that played over and over in his mind.

The murder.

Had the spell been broken? Would tonight be different?

Light blasted through the small opening and Louis rushed to the wall. Heavy thuds of pounding feet grew closer. On the other side, the man he had seen on the other occasion rushed toward him.

Is this the man who will free me?

The twelfth bell struck midnight and the light disappeared from the wall, as abruptly as if a curtain had been draped over a window to shut out sunlight.

He plunged once again into his black hell.

Kirby
Portsmouth, Virginia Present Day

The woman who checked Kirby into Clothiste's Inn earlier said she would be on the premises all night, but he was to come and go as he wished.

She pointed out where to find coffee and tea, then beckoned him to follow her through the dining room to the parlor, where the room temperature was comfortable and cozy. No mysterious mists slithered around their feet. Kirby felt a bit sheepish that he had even looked. As they headed toward the staircase to the upstairs suites, he stared into the antique mirror over the mantle, willing the figure he had once seen to reappear.

Only his own features glanced back.

He settled his belongings in his room and went straight back downstairs. He could hear the evening newscast blaring from the direction of the innkeeper's room.

The colonial-styled parlor remained innocuous, the warm blues in the furniture welcoming. Ignoring Terry's warning from the night before, he even moved the forbidden candlesticks from one side to the other, hoping to see some paranormal activity.

Despite his insistence that he didn't believe in ghosts or

other-worldly apparitions, a mild disappointment washed over him.

He headed for dinner at the Bier Haus, planning to return before midnight to check the mirror.

But he'd run into a group of friends and hadn't realized how much time had passed. At quarter to twelve, he dashed out of the restaurant and raced back to the B and B.

Kirby turned the key in the kitchen door and stepped over the threshold. Trying to be as quiet as possible, he closed the door.

The mantle clock in the parlor tolled the first stroke of midnight. The single peal echoed with a mournful resound. The second gong sounded. Kirby closed the door and turned the key, flinching at the click that sounded like the turning of an empty gun cylinder reverberating throughout the room. The third toll echoed.

Under his breath, Kirby counted with the clock as he moved forward.

Four.

Each subsequent gong of the clock seemed to ring louder and longer than the previous, the rush of his pulse pounding in his ears. A light over the stove illuminated his path.

Five.

He navigated around the cooking island and the counters.

Six.

Next, he passed through the dining room, backlit by a light in the parlor. Not the low golden lamplight he'd left burning, but a wavering green swath of light glowed ahead of him.

Seven.

He quickened his pace while trying to keep quiet. Despite his efforts, he bumped against a curio cabinet. Bric-a-brac jostled, and the glass door jolted open.

Eight.

He placed his hands against the cabinet door to settle the rattling glass.

Nine.

Kirby moved to the doorway separating the dining room

and parlor.

Ten.

Low light emanated from a small table lamp. Kirby glanced at the mantle and stopped short. The mirror emitted a greenish cast, the glass rippling with waves.

Eleven.

His gaze remained locked on the shimmering mirror. The hands of the clock just below whirled backwards, passing each other over and over. The single peal seemed to last for minutes. The reverberation pierced his ears, the jangle coursing from his head to his feet. He thundered forward, hand outstretched to the ghost-like face he saw appearing through the vacillating glass.

"Don't move!" A voice shouted behind him, startling him as much as the scene he had just witnessed.

Twelve.

The green light disappeared, and the room plunged into pitch black for a split second before light from the chandelier flooded the room.

Kirby whirled on one heel to face the barrel of a pistol aimed straight at him, center mass.

Sandi's eyes widened, but with rock-steady hands she lowered the .45, thumb switching the safety on.

"Kirby? I thought you were a burglar." She slipped the gun into her housecoat pocket, jaw taut. She relaxed her shoulders. "I heard the noise and saw your form moving from the dining room."

"What are you doing here? Where's the lady who checked me in?"

"She called Terry about nine and said she heard crying ghosts and wasn't staying another minute in this place. Terry and the girls were in Richmond at some wedding show Stephanie wanted to go to, so they asked if I could come to the inn."

"Well, I'm glad you aren't trigger-happy," Kirby gasped, hand rubbing his chest. He wasn't sure his heart could stand much more strain tonight. His gaze dropped to the pistol. "Do you really know how to use that gun?" He clenched his jaw and winced. "And sorry for that very sexist remark."

Sandi shrugged. "I grew up around guns, have been handling them since I was a kid. I started carrying after Terry was attacked a few weeks ago. Sorry to scare you."

"Did you see what just happened?" Kirby asked. He inclined his head toward the fireplace.

"See what? What do you mean?"

"That greenish glow from the mirror, did you see that? Or the crazy way the hands of the clock circled backwards?" Kirby pointed to the two innocuous items sitting in their respective places above the fireplace.

Sandi shook her head.

"You didn't see that?" Kirby frowned. "Or the shimmers in the mirror?"

Sandi repeated the negative motion.

"The clock chiming midnight. Did it seem like each gong seemed to last longer and louder?"

"Kirby, are you drunk?" Sandi took a step closer to him and sniffed.

"I had a couple—okay maybe three beers—during dinner. In fact, I'll even admit I've had more beers this month than I think I've had in my whole life. But no, I'm not drunk. I just saw something weird." Kirby plopped on the couch and leaned back, scrubbing his hands over his eyes.

"Look, I'm going to put on some coffee, and you're going to tell me what happened, what you saw." Sandi flicked the wall switch to turn off the chandelier. Shadows lengthened in the lower lighting from the table lamp.

"I don't want to discuss it." Kirby leaned forward, elbows on knees.

"Well, that's too bad, Doc. I'm a lawyer. Nothing you say can surprise me. I've already heard about all the peculiar things that have happened to Terry and the others in these buildings. I've never seen anything, but I know Terry and her family, and they are stalwart people. Things have occurred, and sometimes involves the little kids. My daughter is asleep in my room, so I want to know what happened here tonight, to know whether it's safe for her to be with me."

"Let me ask you this, Sandi. Does Norrie speak French?"

"French? Other than to name a pastry or two at the café, no. Why do you ask?"

"Make that coffee extra strong," Kirby ordered. "And we'll talk."

***

Sandi set the tray with creamer, sugar, two cups, and a full pot of coffee on the table. She filled the cups and pushed one toward Kirby before pouring milk in hers. Kirby drank his black and he leaned back as Sandi sat at the opposite end of the couch. She tucked one leg under as she settled.

"Let me explain a little bit,' he began. "I've felt an unusual interest in this house ever since I jogged past it while it was being renovated. As soon as I knew it was available for guests, I booked the weekend for me and Liana, so we were invited to the open house celebration."

"At the costume party." Sandi nodded. "I remember seeing you dressed as a colonial soldier, but I don't remember seeing anyone with you."

Kirby shook his head. "Liana didn't come that night. She thought the idea of staying in the B and B when I lived so close was crazy. Anyway, I went alone, and as I walked to the building that night, I kept hearing the wind in the trees. I could have sworn someone was calling a name, drawing out the word 'Lou-wee.' I arrived at the same time as Tanner and his parents. He's a little pistol but was really raising a fuss about dressing like a drummer boy. After I'd been there a while, he came over to me to see my ring." Kirby twirled the emerald on his finger. "I picked him up and asked him if he was having fun. He saluted and said 'Aye, aye, sir.'"

Sandi shifted as Kirby sipped his coffee. He continued. "But he wasn't talking to me. He was looking into the mirror. The glass shimmered, and our images changed before the mirror returned to normal. I really thought they had some kind of Halloween hologram rigged up. But later…" Kirby paused.

"Something happened later?" Sandi asked.

With a nod, Kirby scrubbed his hands over his face. "This sounds so ludicrous. I don't believe I'm even talking about it." He looked at Sandi's receptive face and continued. "I finally had another chance to look at the mirror. I saw just the man this time, alone, in a British soldier's uniform. I touched the mirror at the same time the image moved, and his hand reached through the glass and his fingers touched my hand." He looked at his ring again. "He wore a ring almost identical to mine, but it had blood on it. Almost as soon as it appeared, the hand disappeared. I felt as if I'd just come from out of a trance. I looked around the room. None of the party-goers seemed to have noticed anything amiss, but I remember what song was playing."

"What was it?"

Kirby gave a wry smile. "Would you believe 'I Put a Spell on You' was just finishing?"

"Gotta love Creedence." Sandi drew an afghan over her legs and settled.

"I thought the same thing. I also thought I was losing my frigging mind. Everyone went on about their business, but I stood there, waiting for something else to happen. And guess what song played next?

Sandi shrugged. "No clue."

"Wilson Picket's 'In the Midnight Hour.'"

"You're kidding."

"I'm not. I took it as some sort of message, and I have been dying to get back here ever since. This evening at dinner I ran into some friends and it slipped my mind. Maybe midnight had some significance. Just as I walked into the inn, the clock started to toll. It seemed like each gong stretched out, and I thought the room took on a greenish hue. The mirror looked like ripples of water were washing over it, but the clock hands just twirled counterclockwise in this crazy spin. And that was it."

Silence dangled in the air. Sandi's eyebrows arched, and she shook her head. "I can't offer any explanations about what you've just told me, but I'm used to hearing similar stories from Terry and her family. I know you're a surgeon, so I doubt you'd be given to flights of fancy. Like I said, I never experienced anything myself. I feel perfectly safe here, comfortable even. But if anything would put Norrie in danger, I'd be out of here in a second. You asked me if she spoke French. What made you ask that?"

"The first time I met her was when she and Tanner ran into the café after their dress rehearsal. She looked like a little colonial girl doll I once bought for a cousin's young daughter. What are they called? American Dolls?"

"American Girl, but I knew what you meant."

"Oh, okay. Anyway, Norrie came running in after Tanner, skidded up to me and whispered, '*Bonsoir*, Louis.' Like the other times I've heard the name pronounced with a French accent, she emphasized the 'Lou-wee.'"

Sandi pondered for a minute before shaking her head. "I have no idea where that came from. She's learned some Spanish from watching *Dora the Explorer* but that's about it." She glanced toward the bedroom. "She was so excited we were staying here tonight. She loves this place. All of the properties, actually, including my office building. If I had not birthed her myself, I would swear she belonged here. But other than my friendship with Terry, we are not connected to the family."

"How about your husband? Was he related to the family?"

"No, but I never married Norrie's father," Sandi said. "We were college sweethearts and dated our junior year. I got pregnant and he bolted like the coward he is. His family is mega-millions rich and they sent him to some resort they own in Tahiti, where he took up surfing. He's been loafing there in the sun and sea ever since. They offered to pay off my student loans if I had an abortion. I refused, obviously, and his parents wanted nothing to do with me or the baby. We had some pretty nasty exchanges, but eventually they all agreed to terminate their rights and never have contact with us again, if I did not name their son on Norrie's birth certificate or try to collect child support. I had no problem with either of those conditions. I told them to pack sand and Norrie and I have been on our own ever since."

Kirby stretched his bad leg and rubbed along the side of his calf, wincing at the stiffness.

Sandi poured more coffee in her cup, then hovered the pot over his. "More?" Kirby nodded, and she continued. "Your turn. How did you hurt your leg, if you don't mind my asking?"

"Turnabout is fair play," Kirby said with a laugh. He sobered instantly. "I deployed with a team to Afghanistan. We were moving from one FOB—Forward Operating Base—to another, when a horrific traffic accident occurred right in front of our convoy, involving a school bus and a taxi. We got clearance to stop and offer medical assistance. A local truck loaded with wood poles turned the corner. When the driver saw the accident, he swerved, and the load shifted. He lost control. Boards were flying everywhere as the truck flew over the bumps in the broken road. One of the boards worked to the side like a bouncing airplane wing." Kirby stretched one arm straight out and dipped his hand to simulate the motion. He told Sandi the story he had relayed to the injured sailor. "I got clipped in the lower back just below the flak jacket. The impact shattered my pelvis and thighbone, a few other less serious broken bones and some assorted internal injuries."

"Oh, my God, how awful." Sandi's left hand went to her throat and she clutched her housecoat lapel with the other, knuckles turning white.

"They managed to save my life and eventually got me stateside. With this type of injury, you are immobilized, flat on your back, while this device holding your bones together protrudes from your body like some kind of kid's building set. I had months of rehabilitation and therapy and recovered. I was able to remain in the Navy. I even got back to jogging, albeit much slower and a bit awkward at times. I have a patient in the hospital with injuries similar to mine. He was pretty despondent today about how his injuries will affect his life—his job, his relationship with his girl, his future. I hope I gave him some insight. He'll never recover one hundred percent, but I think he will be able to resume a normal life. It takes time to recuperate, and hopefully his girlfriend will stand by him until he reaches that point. Some relationships make it through such a crisis, others don't."

"Were you engaged when you had your accident?" Sandi blurted out the words before she could stop them. She shifted and apologized. "I'm sorry. My lawyer's mind sometimes kicks in too soon." *And it's my woman's heart that wants to know the answer.*

Kirby nodded. "I was. A few months after the engagement, I was deployed. When I got home, Liana stayed by my side for the first two months. She brought store-bought goodies for the staff. She loved the attention, not only from the male staff, but from patients who admired her good looks, no matter how injured they were."

"But she stayed with you while you made it through your recovery."

Kirby leaned back on the couch and sighed. "She did. Liana always liked the idea of being the fiancée of a doctor, but we just never made it to the altar. We kept putting off setting a date. But she is into perfection, and over time, my scars, which are pretty graphic, reminded her that I was not. She began to turn her eyes away, couldn't look at me anymore. Recently I caught her with another man."

Sandi reached out and touched Kirby's arm. "Kirby, it was thoughtless of me to dredge up painful memories. I'm so sorry."

"It's okay." Kirby smiled. "Talking to Trevor at the hospital already did all that. I talked to him about my injuries and recovery to give him hope, that he can recuperate and return to a normal life, but I did not tell him about my engagement. The last thing he needs to worry about is whether his girl might not be able to see past the physical scars. I met his mother and she seems to think that the girlfriend will stick by him through thick and thin."

The clock struck one. He and Sandi glanced in the direction of the fireplace mantle.

When nothing happened, Kirby stood. "Well, all the hype I was expecting for the midnight hour didn't come to pass." He laughed. "Maybe it was all in my imagination after all."

"Well, speaking of imagination, how's your Christmas spirit?" Sandi asked.

"My what?"

"Your Christmas spirit. Norrie and I are going to Busch Gardens for the Christmas Town event. We go every year. Would you like to come with us? I know she would love that." Sandi loaded the tray with their empty cups.

"Hmm." Kirby mulled the idea in his mind as he and Sandi walked to the hallway at the base of the stairway. "I haven't been to Busch Gardens in years."

"Well, we have to fix that. What do you say, will you come with us?"

"Sure. It sounds like fun."

"Then I need to get some sleep. She's already set the alarm for seven. Your breakfast at the café is included in your rate, you know. We can meet there. We should be on the road by eight."

Kirby leaned forward and brushed Sandi's cheek with a chaste kiss. "See you in a few hours." He walked up the stairs to his suite, wondering what had possessed him to tell Sandi of his flaws.

Sandi, meantime, carried the tray to the kitchen, thinking Kirby Lawrence was the most perfect man she had ever met.

CHAPTER 13

"I Had the Time of My Life"

By the end of a long day at the amusement park, Sandi's impression of Kirby as the perfect man became etched in stone.

He displayed endless patience with Norrie's efforts to see and touch everything in the Christmas setting, and endured the long waits for her to ride every ride in the children' section. When Norrie begged to be taken on an intimidating-looking roller coaster, Sandi explained that she was not yet tall enough, sending the little girl into a pout.

Kirby scooped her into his arms and she buried her face in his neck. He asked, "Is this a Harry Potter ride?"

Norrie raised her head and looked askance. She and her mother burst into laughter.

"What's so funny? What did I say?"

Between giggles, Norrie explained with all the wisdom of a well-read kid. "Harry Potter was in 'Gryffindor House.' This ride is called 'Griffon.' They're not the same thing at all."

"Oh, I see." Kirby winked at Sandi over Norrie's shoulder. "Now I have an idea. What do you say we save Griffon the roller coaster until the summer, when you might be a whole lot bigger? I have it on good authority that kids grow much bigger in the summertime."

"Who says?"

In a stage whisper, Kirby said, "Santa," sending Norrie into a new round of laughter.

"Can we go have peppermint fudge hot chocolate?" The little girl buffed her nose against Kirby's in an Eskimo kiss. The gesture warmed his heart and brought a tear to Sandi's eyes.

Kirby cleared his throat and managed to say, "Sure. But I'm starved. Let's try the Christmas dinner first."

"Like all the other families?" Norrie scooted from Kirby's arms, and while still holding one of his hands, she grabbed her mother's and settled between them.

"It'll be dark when we get done," Sandi said over the lump in her throat. "After we eat, we'll come out and see all the lights twinkling and twirling."

"Yay!" As Norrie tugged them through the throng, Kirby kept his face straight ahead, but he could not resist the urge to glance to Sandi on his left. She looked ahead too, and turned to him, eyes wide.

"Do you mind?" She nodded toward Norrie's hand in his.

Kirby met her gaze. "Not at all."

Crowds seemed to part as the trio continued their walk past animated displays. The multitudes of overhead lights sent colors dancing in their path.

More than one heart in that trio exploded in time with the Christmas music.

***

After an early dinner, Kirby and Sandi sat on a park bench while Norrie rode a carousel of pint-sized Clydesdales in the Scottish country section. Sometimes the lines were so short she could get back in the queue for another spin, giving the two adults ample time to talk in relaxed, comfortable conversation. Sandi's admiration for Kirby continued to grow the longer they spent time together. In spite of the adverse situation in which Kirby had found his fiancée, he did not bash her. Although the humiliation Kirby must have suffered made her want to claw the witch's eyes out in his defense, she admired his dignity and lack of ill will.

When Norrie skipped to their bench and asked if she could ride the "Li'l Clydes" one more time, Sandi called out, "Only once more. We want to go see some shows too."

"Yes, Momma!" Norrie danced her way back to the line to wait.

"She is a sweet little kid,"

"She is." Her eyes lit up.

Kirby recalled Sandi's explanation of Norrie's dad abandoning them to surf in Tahiti, and his family severing all ties with Sandi. "Her dad doesn't know what he's missing."

"You mean her sperm donor?" Sandi practically spat the words. "I hope a damn cobra or something venomous bites the asshole."

"The donor's or the snake's?" Kirby asked, eyes twinkling.

"What?" Sandi stared until she caught on to the joke.

"Well, come to think of it, the *gluteus maximus* would be a wonderfully tender spot for a snake to bite, but on the other hand, I'm not sure there are any poisonous snakes in Tahiti."

Sandi laughed, and shook her head. "Maybe not. Still, he would deserve that and more. It's better for us that he is out of our lives, but I'd go through every bit of misery again that bastard put me through to have Norrie in my life." Her gaze drifted toward her daughter. "How about you, though? Have you ever wanted kids?"

Kirby paused, eyes on Norrie sailing by on her little Clydesdale. She waved, and he saluted in return.

"I do someday." Kirby twisted and leaned his elbow on the back of the bench, cupping his chin in his hand. "I suppose that's a subconscious reason why Liana and I never set a wedding date. Besides the fact that we each had full careers and it just wasn't a good time for children in our lives, I don't think she ever really wanted kids. Do you ever think you'll want any more?"

Sandi lifted a shoulder. "I don't think there will ever be any more for me. I love my baby girl but..."

"Well, it's over for me and Liana. I don't know what my future holds. Time will tell."

She glanced at Kirby from the corner of her eye and her heart pattered in little flip-flops. She could fall in love with this man so easily. The realization struck Sandi like a thunderbolt. She wasn't looking for love. She hadn't even been on a date since Norrie's birth. And she'd been fine with that. Her child was her world, and combined with a hectic law practice, she'd had little time for anything else.

But something felt different whenever she was in Kirby's presence. Her gaze often drifted to him, and whenever they came into contact, she didn't draw away from him like she normally did.

Maybe if we can spend just a little more time together we could move forward.

She looked over to Kirby, wishing she could read his thoughts, and found his gaze locked on her.

By then, Norrie had returned. Satisfied with her cycle of rides, she took the adults by the hand to lead the way to the next area of the park.

***

Lighter than normal traffic on the route home meant a shorter than normal drive to the inn. Kirby carried a sleeping Norrie to the innkeeper's room, and at Sandi's direction, he set the little girl on the bed and met Sandi where she waited by the door.

Both exhausted from the long day, they leaned on opposite sides of the door frame and looked at each other. "I'll get her settled in her p.j.'s in a minute. Thank you so much for joining us today, Kirby," Sandi added, crossing her arms. "Norrie had a wonderful time."

Kirby mirrored her movement. "I really had fun too. She's

a great little kid."

"Sometimes I worry that she's missing a lot, being raised by a single parent."

"She's fine. It's obvious you're doing a good job."

They remained in place, silence broken by the clock chiming ten o'clock. Kirby glanced toward the parlor.

"I guess whatever vibes I was getting about midnight being important were all in my head," he said with a rueful chuckle. "I really thought I was going to see something last night."

"Well, at least you know you checked it out and now you can move on."

"That's true."

They stayed in place a minute more. Sandi made the first move. She leaned forward and brushed a kiss on his cheek. "Goodnight, Kirby." She smiled but remained close to him.

Straightening away from the doorframe, Kirby tilted her chin and brought their mouths together. The taste of warm peppermint chocolate danced on their lips. As the kiss deepened, Sandi slid her arms to rest on Kirby's chest. His heart thudded under her fingertips.

It was just the one kiss. They stepped apart and touched their foreheads together.

"Goodnight," she whispered, voice catching in her throat.

"Goodnight," he repeated. He leaned forward and nuzzled her nose with his before going to his room.

He kicked off his shoes and threw his coat on the coat rack behind the overstuffed chair. He sank into the comfortable cushions and lifted his feet to the ottoman.

It was just the one kiss. He closed his eyes, reliving the memory of that one kiss, every nerve in his body stimulated.

He didn't know whether he was ready to get back into the dating world—or if he even wanted to. Then he remembered walking under the multi-colored lights with Norrie's hand tight in his, and her mother on the other side.

"Like all the other families?" The little girl's voiced echoed over and over as he fell asleep.

***

Kirby's kiss lingered on Sandi's lips. She tried to ignore the tingle where their mouths touched, concentrating instead on helping her sleepy daughter change into nightclothes. Norrie snuggled with her doll under one arm and settled down. Sandi tucked the covers around the child and kissed her goodnight.

Norrie thrust the doll under her nose. "Kiss Maggie goodnight too." Sandi obliged and kissed her daughter's favorite doll, which was costumed in colonial clothing. Although the toy figure had come with its own name, Norrie had insisted on calling her Maggie. Sandi had no idea how Norrie had come up with Maggie, but she'd gone along with it.

She had climbed more hills and walked more steps at Busch Gardens than she had in ages, and every muscle in her legs paid her back for not exercising more often. Stretching to ease the throbbing pain in her bones, Sandi headed to the bathroom to brush her teeth and wash up for the night.

Over a mouth full of toothpaste, she stared in the mirror. Telltale half-dollar blushes marked each cheek.

"It was just a good night kiss," she said aloud. "Don't make it more than it was."

Still, she smiled at the memories of their day at the amusement park as she removed her makeup. This had to be one of the best days of her life. After a laid-back breakfast, they had arrived to find entry lines pleasantly short. In spite of Norrie's sulk at not being tall enough to ride some of the rides, Kirby had handled it without missing a beat. Later, when they'd come across a street skit in the Hastings section of the park, he'd sent Norrie into peals of laughter when he hoisted her on his shoulders to watch the festivities.

"Mommy!" Pure fear echoed in the tiny voice and Sandi was no longer strolling through memories from the amusement park but jerked back to reality. She dropped her facecloth and rushed into the bedroom, shouting, "I'm here, baby."

She glanced at the bed. The soft light from the lamp near

the headboard cast a warm glow on her daughter's face, serene in peaceful sleep. Even Sandi's shouts had not disturbed the child.

Sandi's gaze darted to every corner of the room. She opened the door to the closet. Empty clothes hangers shifted with the movement of air, but the space stood empty. She shut the door and moved to the main bedroom, listening before turning the lock and peering into the hall.

Finding nothing amiss, she locked it again.

She must have called out in her sleep. Sandi changed to yoga pants and a t-shirt, moving mechanically, all the while keeping her gaze on her daughter.

Her heart thumped as a cold shiver iced down her back. For some inexplicable reason, she recalled Stephanie reading the old family letters about the little girl who had vanished and never been found. She crawled into the bed and cradled her daughter in her arms. She lay there, listening to her racing heartbeat slow to a normal pattern as her watch ticked the passing seconds.

Upstairs, floorboards creaked as Kirby moved about his room. Two muffled thuds followed by silence told Sandi he had probably kicked his shoes off on the rug and settled into his bed.

Her gaze drifted upwards, the sizzle of his kiss returning to her lips. Her cheeks warmed.

It was just one kiss.

That last thought was still on her mind as she drifted to sleep.

CHAPTER 14

"My Grandfather's Clock"

1st Toll of Midnight
Portsmouth present, Portsmouth past

The faraway sounds of a sobbing child broke through Kirby's sleep. He raised his head to hear better. *Did I just dream that?*

Silence. He scrambled from the canopied four-poster and slipped to his bedroom door to listen. *Could it have been Norrie having a bad dream?* He strained his ears but heard nothing.

He opened his bedroom door and waited. He heard nothing further but wanted to check the first floor. The stairs creaked each time a foot touched a tread. He reached the foot of the staircase and stared around the dim parlor, lit by the small table lamp that always burned at night. He turned to take the short hall to the innkeeper's suite when a pinpoint of green light caught the corner of his eye. He glanced toward the mirror. Minute sparkles of electric green light danced around the shadowy figure outlined in the glass.

Sharp clicks resounded in the otherwise silent parlor as the antique clock on the mantle signaled the passing of each minute. The shorter arrow had two minutes left before the pair of hands would join straight up at the stroke of midnight.

A quick glance at Sandi's door revealed no light reflected within. The hall was silent. Kirby strode across the parlor and turned the three-way bulb in the table lamp to a higher watt, brightening the room. The mirror appeared normal, his image and the view behind him crystal clear. He took a stance in front of the fireplace, arms crossed. The two silver candlesticks maintained sentry-like positions at either end of the mantle. The clock clicked again as it marked off the fifty-ninth minute of the hour. He brushed his fingers across the mirror, the glass cool and solid to the touch.

The shorter, arrow-shaped hand moved and wavered under the number 12, jerking side to side as if invisible forces fought to keep the hour and minute indicators apart. The timepiece shook, its internal chimes clanging in low echoes, the candlesticks rattling in tempo. The two clock arrows resisted the meeting point and began to spin in opposite directions. At the same time, a transparent green glow washed over him.

Kirby's mirrored image melted as the framed glass quivered. Runny waves of grainy black and white reflected back, made eerier by the blaze of green light. He stretched his hand and touched his fingers to the bottom of the frame. His hand plunged to the wrist through the waterfall effect and brushed against something solid on the other side. He pulled his arm back, stunned.

Before he could make another move, the clock struck midnight. A man's image formed. A hand shot through the shimmying glass and clutched Kirby's wrist. Kirby pulled back, but the apparition held firm. They jerked back and forth several times as he fought to free himself, then another outstretched hand broke through the glass and grabbed his shirt.

A tug-of-war ensued as Kirby pulled away. The apparition gained the upper hand and dragged Kirby through the mirror. The grip loosened, and the form disappeared as a twirling vortex sucked Kirby into its wake. His body grew heavier as the speed of the spinning increased.

Blazing beams of red, white, and blue mixed with the green, blinding him. The pinprick lights pulsed in time with the reverberations of the long-sounding chime, sending shockwaves through his body. He struggled to place his hands over his ears to block the piercing clang, but his arms dropped to his sides like lead weights.

His body stretched, skin straining against his bones, his very cheekbones threatening to rip through his face.

The blaze of lights alternated with blackness as he shot through the portal. Doors opened, pulsating lights illuminating the voids behind. Each time he sailed toward one door, the access slammed shut before he entered.

In the next moment Kirby somersaulted headfirst through the air, over and over. The faster he flipped, the lighter his body became. The blinding lights faded, the ringing dwindled in time with the patter of rain.

A solitary door opened in the pitch black. The roar of a thunderstorm reached a deafening crescendo before he was sucked through the entry.

Crash-landing on his butt, Kirby rolled heels-over-head until he ended in a kneeling position. Unsteady, he rocked forward and opened his eyes, his nose inches away from the tip of a colonial sword.

Fortunately, the sword was sheathed in a worn leather scabbard and poked out at an angle from the side of a white-clad thigh. As the soldier shifted, the tip moved closer to Kirby's face. He scuttled backwards in a crab-like scramble, and then struggled to his feet. A pitcher in a basin rattled and steadied as he placed his hand against the table.

His noisy arrival seemed not to have reached the ears of the occupants of the room.

A woman sat propped in a high four-poster bed, a baby in her arms. At her side, a midwife—*now how the hell would I know that*—tucked covers around the obviously new mother.

Kirby looked around. He was in a bedchamber of some sort.

Where the hell am I? And why do I know this place is called a bedchamber and not a bedroom?

The mother settled the blanket around the infant and stroked its cheek. Although she was clothed, Kirby realized the mother was breastfeeding. He looked to the ceiling. As a doctor, he considered the act as natural as breathing, but he also did not wish to intrude on a private family moment.

"Ma chère femme, vous m'avez donné un beau fils. Je t'aime." The soldier leaned down and kissed her forehead. She angled her face until their lips met.

Kirby had never spoken French in his life, but apparently, he did now, as he understood the man telling his wife she had given him a handsome son, and he loved her.

"Mon Étienne, mon amour," she crooned. She stroked his face while her husband, in a move similar to hers, brushed his knuckles across the baby's rosy cheek.

Étienne, Clothiste. *I've heard those names before! Louis' parents? And also the names of twins of later generations?*

He studied the soldier. Étienne wore a uniform consisting of a blue wool jacket trimmed with red cuffs and cross-lapels, and white breeches. He removed the belt holding the saber, swiveling on his heel to set the scabbard at an angle on the wooden stand, and returned to his wife's side. Although Kirby stood only inches away, Etienne neither looked his way nor acknowledged him.

"You have made me a proud man, Clothiste," he said. Still able to understand the conversation, Kirby shifted with the uncomfortable act of eavesdropping. Étienne sat on the edge of the bed. Clothiste kissed the baby's forehead before handing him to his father.

The infant stretched and yawned.

"What's this, my little son? You are bored with your papa already?" The soldier and his wife laughed as they cuddled their baby between them.

The midwife smiled, gathered a pile of linens from a chair nearby and discreetly slipped from the room. She returned moments later carrying a tray with a bottle and glasses. Kirby stepped out of her way, but the woman breezed past him without a nod in his direction.

Am I a ghost? He glanced at his hands and tapped his fingertips together. His skin was solid to his touch. He could feel the callous that had formed below his ring, caused by the way he gripped his briefcase.

He glanced toward the mother and father cooing over their baby. *Are they ghosts?*

"What shall we name our son, my love?" Clothiste asked.

"We must name him Louis after your papa, Clothiste," Étienne replied. "How overjoyed he would have been to know of the birth of his first grandchild."

"I miss Papa so terribly," Clothiste said, voice quivering. "He would be so proud that his first grandson bore his name. Louis." A tear trailed down her face and dropped onto the baby's forehead before she could catch it. "My little Louis Étienne de la Rocher."

"And he is christened before the visiting priest even arrives?" Étienne's voice rang with amusement as he touched the bead of moisture and brought his fingertip to his lips to kiss the glistening droplet. He stroked his wife's cheek. "Such a long name for such a little baby. We must make it easier for him to live in America. We shall simply call him Louis Étienne Rocher. Agreed, *ma cherie?*"

"*Oui*. Father Farmer arrives in Fishkill in two weeks, *mon amour*." Clothiste rested her hand on her husband's shoulder. "The Noel twins are going to receive their first Holy Communion. Now we shall have a baptism to celebrate as well. Who will we seek for godparents?"

"Let us make this an easy decision and ask your sister and her husband."

"Emilie and Eduard shall be thrilled."

Étienne shifted and crossed one booted ankle over the other.

Clothiste's gaze dropped to the shiny leather brushing against her covers and sighed with a smile. Etienne returned the smile, a dimple lining his cheek as he leaned forward to tug off the offending boots. She hugged her child closer. "I hope the war is over soon and our young boy does not have to grow up to be a soldier," she murmured, her lips against the soft fluff on her baby's crown.

He leaned over to kiss his wife's furrowed brow. "My dear, soldiers are needed whether we are at war or not."

As if in agreement, baby Louis stirred and his lips curved.

Étienne laughed. "See, my wife. Our son agrees that he will be a soldier."

A shiver rippled through Clothiste and she drew her shawl tighter. "Let us not talk of such things right now. Shall we hope instead for a life of peace and quiet for our firstborn?"

"You are right, *ma cherie*, and it was thoughtless of me to discuss our son in the army. So, let us decide now the career for our son. Shall he be a farmer, a scholar, or a physician?"

"Those alternatives make me happier than the idea of a soldier," Clothiste said with a laugh. "But in the end, the choice will be his."

Baby Louis yawned and stretched, poking both tiny fists forward, thumbs and forefingers extended in the classic imitation of a pistol. He had made his choice.

The distant peal of a clock chimed, the increasing volume pummeling Kirby's eardrums. His body stiffened as unseen forces tugged on his limbs like the pull of a magnet to metal.

Clothiste glanced toward him and their eyes locked. She nodded once, kind eyes filled with worry.

He was pulled back into the whirlpool of darkness, the endless bell echoing in his ears.

CHAPTER 15

"Caught Somewhere in Time"

2nd Toll of Midnight
Colonial America 1768

Kirby floated through a narrow tunnel, the reverberating bell replaced by shrill whistles as roaring winds tore past his face. His eyes watered from the stabbing air. He clenched his teeth and grimaced in pain at the pulling and twisting of his skin and bones. Doors opened and slammed shut as he hurled forward. A door snapped open. He crashed through an invisible barrier and landed on his butt, his back inches away from a roaring fire. Cold from his twirl in time, he scooted closer to the fire, the warmth radiating along his spine.

In front of him, a family gathered close around a small couch and two wooden chairs. Candles in silver candlesticks filled nearly every space on shelves and tables, casting flickering light along the walls. A woman sat on the couch, stroking the forehead of a sleeping girl of perhaps three or four. At the woman's feet, another girl, older by no more than a year, sat on the floor. She held a small wrapped bundle, her tiny hands caressing the ribbon holding the muslin cover in place.

A man walked to the couch and touched the shoulder of the woman. Kirby recognized them as the same couple he had first seen, holding the newborn infant Louis. Both adults had aged a few years from the first time he had seen them.

Kirby blinked and glanced around. Fresh green sprigs scattered around the bases of several large candle holders on the fireplace mantle. On one side of a low table sat a silver tray with a teapot and four china teacups on saucers; a dish of nuts and berries graced the opposite end. The aroma of roasting meat wafted to his nostrils, mixing with a clove-studded orange on the mantle. His approving stomach growled in anticipation and he rubbed it.

How can I hear, see, and smell yet remain invisible to the others?

A young boy sat cross-legged on the floor, a drum on his lap. His bottom lip protruded in a sulk and his shoulder slumped in dejection.

"A drum? I want to be a soldier, not a drummer. I wanted to have my own rifle."

"*Mon fil*, a drummer is just as important to the army as the soldier with a gun." Etienne leaned down and tapped the drum lightly with a fingertip. "Without the drummer or piper to relay signals from the commanding officer, the garrison would not know how to follow orders. The drumbeats help the soldiers to march in time, tells them when to do certain tasks, or when to fire their weapons."

"But, Papa, when will *Père Noël* bring me a gun?"

Étienne frowned and knelt before his son. "Is this how you show your appreciation for your Christmas gift?

The boy, so like Tanner that Kirby marveled at the uncanny resemblance, lowered his head. "Papa, I am sorry. *Merci pour mon tambour.* Thank you. I am very happy with it." He brightened. "I already know the signals for both the Americans and the British armies. Watch me." Louis tapped out a series of sharp beats. "This is the American signal."

Étienne raised one eyebrow. "And that is the order for...?"

Louis held a drumstick like a pistol and said, "Fire!" He

mimicked a gunshot. "I shot a redcoat!"

Clothiste frowned and drew her shawl tighter about her shoulders. "Is it not *Noël*, my husband and son? Must we talk of war and army on this special night?"

Étienne knelt in front of his wife and took her hands in his. "*Cherie*, it is but a small gift we talk about."

"It is Christmas, *mon amour*. Is it not enough that we lost our fight in Canada, and left behind our home and everything we love in Acadia? If not for the goodness of your friends who have given us this temporary home, who knows where we would be this Yuletide? Our families have scattered to France, to Louisiana, even to the Caribbean. And what of the poor souls forced to drift on the seas because no one will take them?" Clothiste tightened her grip on Étienne's hands. "These protestors proclaiming 'no taxation without representation' frighten me. All of these efforts to tax the colonies have caused so much unrest. America is headed for a great war and you will be there with them. Yes, my love, it is only a small gift, but as Louis is the son of a soldier, so he will too soon follow in his father's footsteps."

"I will, *Maman*! I will lead the Americans into battle!" Louis rapped the drumsticks and pivoted on his foot.

"But not today, *mon fil*. You must put aside the drum for now." Étienne guided Louis to a seat beside his mother. "It is time for your sister to open her gift. Now, Theresé, it is your turn."

The little girl nodded, chestnut brown hair pulled from her face and secured with a bow. With painstaking care, she untied the ribbon and unrolled the muslin. Her eyes opened wide as she discovered the doll inside.

"A baby! *Pierre Noël* has brought me my own baby!" Theresé hugged the toy to her chest as gently as if she held a glass doll. "She is *tres belle*."

The family allowed time for Theresé to marvel at the small wooden doll with painted face and brown yarn hair, linen dressing gown and white bonnet.

"Do you like my baby" she asked. She showed the doll, first

to her mother, then to her father. At her urging, each parent kissed the forehead of the doll, but when she offered the small face to Louis, he grimaced and poked it with a drumstick. Theresé took her index finger and jabbed him in the shoulder. "Don't hurt my baby," she warned with narrowed eyes.

The two youngsters faced off in a showdown, but their father stepped between them before a new war started. Étienne glanced toward the clock on the mantle. He drew Clothiste to her feet. "It is nearly time for *Le Réveilllon de Noël*. Louis, very quietly, as baby Marie Josephé sleeps, lead us to the dining table where your *maman* has prepared our special midnight meal to celebrate the beginning of Christmas."

Louis slipped the drum straps over his shoulders. Back erect, face solemn, he tapped the sticks in a gentle pattern as he paraded around the room. Theresé marched behind, clutching the doll to her chest. The small family circled in front of Kirby, so close he took a step back, closer to the mantle of the fireplace, the boughs of an evergreen limb scratching the back of his neck.

How can I feel heat, and the touch of the pine branch, but they do not see me? Kirby reached a hand out to move the branch back in place. *How can I smell the scent of this evergreen?*

Clothiste sighed, then placed her arm around Étienne's waist. He angled her in front of him and looked up with a gleam in his eye. Clothiste followed his gaze and smiled at the sprig of mistletoe he held over her head. He tucked two fingers under her chin and tilted her face toward his.

"*Mon amour*, the children!" she admonished.

"*Oui*. Shall we practice how to make a new one?" As if on cue, Marie Josephé whimpered, and drifted back to sleep.

"Foolish man. We have a young one who protests your suggestion." But Clothiste shifted her arms across his shoulders and brushed his lips with a kiss. Eyes twinkling, she nuzzled his ear and whispered, "But practice is always a good idea."

Louis finished his march around the table and re-entered the parlor on tiptoe. With a last gentle clack of the drumsticks, he set the drum down and wedged between his parents, clutching their waists with his arms. Theresé filled in the opposite space at their hips, her fingertips reaching her brother's.

"*Je'taime, j'etaime,*" he cried.

"*Moi aussi!*" Theresé added.

Etienne lifted a child in each arm, and he and Clothiste took turns kissing their cheeks.

The arrows of the mantle clock clicked into place, pointing to twelve. The chime tolled the start of midnight. Louis glanced over his father's shoulder, looked Kirby in the eye and nodded once.

The scene shrunk to a pinpoint before Kirby's vision turned black.

The whirlwind spinning began anew.

CHAPTER 16

"Strange Times"

3rd Toll of Midnight
Portsmouth, Virginia Present Day

Panic coursed through Sandi's veins. She couldn't find Norrie anywhere. A long gloomy corridor stretched before her, and she raced from wall to wall, trying to locate her daughter behind an endless row of doors. In the darkness, the outline of light was visible underneath some of the portals, but every time she reached for the handle, the doorway disappeared, and she moved to the next. In the distance a clock chimed.

A muffled whimper grew into childish sobs, gripping her mother's heart in terror. She forced her mind to drag through her subconscious and awoke with a start, squinting against the bathroom light shining into her eyes. She thrust the covers away to reach for her daughter.

Norrie slept peacefully beside her, each short breath ending in a raggedy little snore. Her serene face displayed no distress. Sandi scooped her daughter into her lap and clutched her against her thundering heart.

While Sandi waited for her heartbeats to return to normal, she tried to shake the gut-wrenching fear that had gripped her during the dream. The subliminal panic had been every bit as real as her conscious. She had always harbored a secret fear that Norrie's father or grandparents would try to snatch her away, and she had watched her daughter like a hawk. The trepidation had lessened once Norrie's father and his parents had given up all rights, but she never gave up her vigilance.

She thought back to Thanksgiving, when she first heard of the poor Lauralee, the Lawrence ancestress whose daughter had disappeared during the 1860s. During the entire time Stephanie had read the letter describing the child's disappearance, Sandi's stomach had been in knots at the very thought of suffering the unimaginable. She wrapped her arms around her daughter and held tight.

Norrie shifted, her clench on Maggie the doll tightening. She snuggled in her mother's arms, thrusting the doll's sharp little hand into Sandi's stomach.

After moving the plastic limb that threatened to become a surgical intrusion into her bladder, Sandi glanced at her watch to see the time.

A full minute passed before she moved, trying to resist the call of nature. Well, I'm sure Miss Maggie's little poke triggered that. *She rubbed her tummy and finally gave up the resistance. She left the door between the bedroom and bathroom partially open as she answered the call.*

Kirby
Somewhere, Winter 1773

Kirby's out-of-control spinning jolted to an end when he landed in a sitting position, in two feet of water covered with a thin layer of ice. The sheet of frozen river cracked into jagged spears. He gasped as the freezing cold splashed his face and pierced his skin. A horse's snorting muzzle blew a spray of chilling water into Kirby's ear. He turned to the left to stare into the baleful eyes of a brown gelding. The horse lowered his head and returned to slurping the ice-cold water.

"*Lever le camp!*" A male voice. "Break camp." The shouts were repeated, the mix of French and English echoing across the small lake Kirby had landed in. Murmuring adult voices mixed with the occasional high pitch of a child shouting and the clangs of metal on metal.

A thin woman poured water on an open campfire, the hiss of liquid meeting flame punctuating the air. The smoky scent blending with the smell of meat drippings drifted to Kirby's nose, reminding him of his hunger. *Cold, wet, hungry. What else can go wrong?* As if reading Kirby's mind, the horse whinnied and splattered his face with more warm breath and icy drops of water.

"*Lever le camp!*" Break camp. Accepting that he was now a Francophone, Kirby listened to the cry repeated over and over.

A man closer to the water's edge took up the initial order, shouting first in French, then in English. "Break camp. The British are four hours behind us. Act fast." Kirby peered around the horse's body. On the far side of the camp, an unseen drummer tapped out a short tattoo, duplicating the beats every few seconds. Men and women scurried along the shore, in orderly and purposeful movements, loading parcels and barrels in wagons. Even children helped, picking up small pots and kettles, passing them in a line to an adult stacking property in carts.

Kirby counted twenty uniformed soldiers, with women, children, and a few men in civilian clothes doubling that number. *Camp followers?* The small army community made short work of clearing the campsite of almost all evidence of their occupation. Even the fire pit had been well covered in fresh dirt. Only wheel marks in flattened grass and ruts in the field indicated where the camp had been.

Soldiers brought four horses to a single file of limbers, two-wheeled carts loaded with artillery and ammunition chests. After harnessing the animals, the soldiers led other horses to the wagons and carts that transported the rest of the camp supplies.

The same soldier who had called in French and English splashed through the water to grab the bridle of the loose steed to turn him around. Kirby moved to the right as the haunches of the big horse brushed his left cheek, but not quick enough to avoid the swish of tail that sent an icy slap of horsehair to his temple and into his ear. Each step the horse took sent a wave of water crashing further up Kirby's chest. The thin shirt he wore offered little comfort.

Teeth chattering, Kirby knelt. His breath blew out in vapory puffs. Although he figured no one could see him, he crawled through the water on his hands and knees, parallel with the shore. He crept up onto the short, muddy embankment to the back of a wagon loaded with supplies. Little more than a peddler's cart with wooden planks for sides, the conveyance held barrels, pots, pans, and to his relief, animal pelts under a canvas covering.

With a cautious eye on his surroundings, he heaved over the sideboards of the cart and wrapped two furs around him. The musky odor of tanned hide and wet hair did not deter him from bundling under the pelts. He grabbed a third, threw it over his knees and hunkered down under the canvas, praying for the violent shakes to stop rocking his body.

Is this how my life ends? Freezing to death in the eighteenth century? He knew not to fall asleep or hypothermia could set in, but fatigue and the stress on his body overwhelmed his senses. The wagon lurched forward and soon creaked in time to the steady sway. A few scattered shouts rang out, followed by the tap-tapping of a drum.

Kirby closed his eyes—for a minute.

When he woke, the wagon no longer moved. He had no idea how long he'd slept or how far they'd traveled. His clothes were almost dry, the moisture wicked away by the animal hides, but his jeans remained cold and damp in the creases at his knees and thighs. He had a pulsing ache in his left ear.

Footsteps crunched near the back of the wagon, followed by muffled coughing.

"*Mon amour!*" Kirby barely recognized Étienne's voice, anxiety in his mix of French and English. "What is wrong?"

Clothiste's frail response was interspersed with coughing. "'Tis nothing—to concern—yourself, Étienne, only a chill."

"Papa, Mama." Girlish voices shouted as lighter footsteps shuffled to the rear of the cart.

"What is it, Theresé?" Étienne asked.

"We cannot find Louis. The other drummers say they saw him before the caravan started, but now no one has seen him since."

"Have you checked all of the wagons?"

"Yes, Mama, we followed the path for fifteen minutes to see if he had fallen behind. There is no sign of him."

"That is not like him." Etienne raised his voice. "Richard—Captain Beecher, come quick."

"Étienne? What is it?" A man answered in French with a distinct British accent.

"Have you seen Louis? Theresé says they have not seen him since we left camp."

"I have not. We departed in such a hurry that I am surprised more were not left behind. I will ask around, make sure he is not here before we go further."

Clothiste spoke, her voice fraught with worry. "Étienne, we must find him. He is barely ten years of age. It will be nightfall soon, and I fear we will have snow before the sun rises." A new wave of coughing began.

"I will have our son home before the night falls, *mon amour*. Theresé, take your mother, see that she is made warm and comfortable. Mix tea with brandy and honey, if we have any. Captain Beecher and I will search for your brother. Marie Josephé, I will need to borrow a pair of civilian breeches and shirt from someone." Marie Josephé gathered her skirts and raced to do her father's bidding.

"If they find you, they will take you," Clothiste said.

"Only if I speak would they know. Theresé has taught me to say 'thank you' in perfect English, so if I must speak, that is all I will say. Richard will handle his countrymen."

Captain Beecher returned. "He is not here, Étienne. One of the children said that Louis was sending signals on the drum and went toward the bushes near the water. He assumed Louis needed to relieve himself. No one saw him after that."

"We should go now, on horseback. It will be faster."

"No, Étienne, that will not be wise. Even though it will slow us, it is better to take this smallest cart. Louis is clever, he will not give us away, but we must appear as travelers searching for the boy. As long as you do not open your mouth, they will not have a clue we are part of the garrison."

In a matter of minutes, the jerky ride began.

With nothing else to do, Kirby drifted into a fitful sleep until the cart lumbered to a stop. He raised the canvas and peered through the side slats. The waning sun shed enough light to see around the camp. Five small tents were angled around a fire pit. The smell of the burning firewood and smoke mixed with the pungent smell of tidal marsh.

"There he is." Étienne pointed toward a small table. Louis sat on the edge, legs dangling. His small, tattered drum was at his side. Two redcoats flanked him, laughing with the young boy.

"Papa!" Louis shouted with a wave.

Richard jumped down and ran to the other cart, calling hello as he strode toward the gathering. Étienne remained silent at the reins. Two other soldiers walked to where Louis sat, one glancing toward Etienne, who raised a hand. Voices murmured, but with the pulsing in his ears, Kirby could not make out the words.

Finally, Richard shook hands with the soldiers, and scooped Louis into one arm. He picked up the drum with his other hand.

"Bye," Louis called. "Bye."

Richard set the boy on the seat next to Étienne and scrambled beside him. Étienne made a clicking sound and jerked the reins to turn the horses around.

The wagon plodded along for what seemed like an eternity to Kirby before either man spoke.

Richard said, "They are scouts, looking for American camps. Fortunately, they had enough ale under their belts that they were inclined to believe our story and let us leave without incident."

"His mother will be grateful to know her son is well. Thank you, Richard."

"You would have done the same for me if it had been James who got left behind. I tell you, Étienne, your son is a natural-born mole. When I walked to the table and said my son was lost and I've come for him, Louis never missed a beat. He rushed to greet me, shouting, 'Papa, Papa! I told them you would come in your peddler's wagon.' I knew he was telling me he had told the soldiers he was the son of a peddler. He spoke with such enthusiasm I could have easily believed I was a tinker and he was my own son greeting me. His accent sounds as British as mine."

Louis laughed. "Theresé has taught me how to mimic accents well."

"Tell me how you became separated from the garrison, Louis. You have caused your mother terrible worry and you could have put us all in danger."

"Papa, I am sorry. I did not mean to cause problems. I saw something strange, and I went to investigate. I thought I saw a man near the wagon. I ran to it but did not find him, so I went to look in the woods. I got turned around and by the time I made my way back, everyone was gone. I followed the wheel marks for a while then lost the tracks in a rocky area. Later I came across the British camp in the forest. I tried to hide, but one of the soldiers saw me." Louis ran out of breath, inhaled and faced his father. "Papa, I did tell them my father was a peddler. I told them that we had camped not far from their camp, and I got left behind when we moved on. I told them we often saw French and American soldiers in fields as we traveled although they weren't near here now. I told them the last garrison I saw yesterday had left for Savannah."

Étienne and Richard threw back their heads and roared with laughter. Richard added, "Savannah! Well, if they follow that path, they will be hell and gone from their base."

"Well done, Louis," Étienne said.

"One of them showed me magic tricks." Louis held an empty hand palm out. With a slight twist, he reached to the side of his father's head. When he withdrew his hand, he held a coin.

"A British pound? How did you get so much money?"

Before answering, Louis turned to Richard and repeated the gestures. Then he raised both hands with coins in triumph.

"They bet me that I could not figure out how to do the magic tricks. After I watched them for a few minutes, I performed the magic. Then a second man didn't believe I could do it again., He made another bet. I got his coin as well."

Again, the men shared guffaws and Étienne clapped the boy on the back.

"What happened next, my clever son?"

"I told them the American drummer boys showed me their drum signals and one of them wrote them down." Louis settled the drum on his lap, drumsticks poised.

"*Mon fil*, you did not tell them the Americans' signals, did you?"

In answer, Louis tapped out a series of beats.

Étienne pulled the cart to an abrupt stop. "Louis! That is the signal to fire our weapons."

"Yes, Papa. I know." Louis nodded. His eyes danced with mischief as he smiled, a dimple lining his cheek. "I told them that is our signal to fetch water." The boy tapped out a different pattern of drumbeats.

Richard frowned. "I don't recognize that command, Louis. Do you know it, Étienne?"

After the father shook his head, Louis repeated the series of taps. "That is the British call to fire their weapons." He tap-tapped again. "That is the order to march. If I join the British Army as a drummer, I could make mistakes sometimes with the orders, cause them to have confusion when they march. I want to be a spy for General Washington, Papa. Am I ready?"

"I think you will be ready soon, mon *fil*." Étienne hugged the boy with one arm. Over his head, he and Richard exchanged glances. Richard raised an eyebrow, and an unspoken message passed between them. Étienne nodded and returned his attention to driving the horses.

Kirby shifted as the sway began. He stacked two loose horseshoes together, creating a single clanging sound that vibrated in his ears, resonating through his skull. His vision started to tunnel.

The last thing he saw before the scene shuttered to black

was Louis kneeling over the back of the wagon seat, looking straight into his eyes, mouth agape, one finger pointing.

CHAPTER 17

"Time Travellers"

4th Toll of Midnight
Williamsburg, Virginia 1774

This time, Kirby's trip through time was briefer than the previous, but still accompanied by a cacophony of sounds. Bells, whistles, the screaming of air rushing past, all greeted his entry into the tunnel. He had barely been sucked into the vortex when he shot directly into an open door as if spit from a cannon. He landed in a parachutist's stance, feet thumping on wooden floor and running a few steps before stopping.

A dim buzzing lingered in his ears. He shook his head, but the incessant humming continued. *Maybe I damaged my hearing in the cold water and weather?* He rocked his jaws from side to side and swallowed, to no avail.

Rubbing his throbbing ears, he glanced around. A fireplace, large enough for a man to stand in, lined one wall. Steam rose from a heavy black cauldron hung over the flames. Along the walls, pewter sconces protected by glass hurricane shades held short tallow candles in various heights. More candles in pewter candlesticks, some with the glass shades and others standing free, flickered on the mantle and on rustic wooden tables. A sense of *déjà vu* washed over Kirby. There was something familiar about his surroundings, but he could not put his finger on it.

Roasting meats mixed with the aroma of fresh baked bread served as a reminder that Kirby had not eaten in—*what, nearly 250 years?* He smiled at his own pathetic joke.

Black and white servants of both sexes waited on customers. As far as Kirby could see, the patrons were men in colonial uniform or gentlemen's jackets, ascots, and breeches.

People's mouths moved, animated heads bobbed in conversation, a waiter dropped a porcelain pitcher that shattered two feet from Kirby.

Yes, he could see, but he could not hear the din around him, could only hear the low buzzing running through his ears.

His gaze drifted to a table in a corner near a window, separated from the rest of the diners. His eyes widened as his gaze landed on a much-older Étienne and a more grown Louis—perhaps in his mid-teens—flanking either side of a man in a dark blue army jacket, threads from gold epaulets shaking with each move.

Kirby's heart skipped a beat as he realized his ancestors were in earnest conversation with General George Washington.

Bits and pieces of chattering wafted to his hearing, in broken patterns like interference during a cell phone conversation. He inched closer to the General's table. A serving maid in a plain blue gown and white apron bustled by, her skirts brushing Kirby as she passed. She remained unaware of his presence as she retrieved pewter plates from a sideboard.

A short, plump woman stopped by the General's table with a bottle of wine and the two engaged in a brief talk. She was obviously in charge of the tavern. Her dress was finer than what the serving girls wore, a material Kirby guessed might be satin. Or maybe brocade. *Who the hell knows?* It was some shiny cream-colored material with gold threads creating patterns, and a silky peach-colored ruffle at her wrists that matched some kind of underskirt thing she wore.

The humming in Kirby's ears faded somewhat. He could hear the clank of pewter on the tables, and the chink of porcelain. Spoken words still eluded his hearing, which swished as if he held his head underwater. The woman turned her head and called something to a black male server, her voice garbled. The server nodded and returned moments later with a plate of flat cakes plied high. He handed the dish to the well-dressed woman, who placed it in front of the general and his guests.

Kirby's stomach rumbled again. His hearing may not be working right, but his nose damn sure was. While the father of the country hunched over a parchment scroll, Étienne and Louis leaned forward to follow the traces Washington's fingertip made. Kirby snagged one of the warm cakes. He inhaled the cinnamon apple scent before he wolfed down the cake. He swiped another between snippets of conversation. *Portsmouth…ships…Bay. Rochambeau…south. Yorktown.*

The buzzing increased again. Kirby winced and rubbed his ear, then reached for a third cake.

Louis sat ramrod straight, his intent gaze shifting between the map and the general's face. He turned once to his father and said something. Étienne answered, his face somber. Louis faced the general again and nodded.

Damn, I wish I knew what they were saying! Kirby reached for another cake as he tried in vain to read lips.

The three men stood. Washington clasped Louis' shoulder as they shook hands. Next the general shook Étienne's hand.

Father and son headed toward the door. Kirby moved to follow, grabbing one more cake and stuffing it in his tattered shirt pocket. Washington sat back down and pulled the plate closer. He frowned, then moved his head from side to side and looked under the table for the missing cakes.

Kirby chuckled inwardly and caught up with his ancestors as they removed coats from hooks and walked out the door.

Snowflakes twirled in the waning daylight. A thin layer already covered the steps. Kirby followed the imprints Louis had left and he joined the father and son on the walkway.

Another wave of *déjà vu* returned, but now Kirby knew why. Although the streets and buildings were quite different, he recalled a visit he had made to Colonial Williamsburg—in the 21st century. After touring the restored area, he and Liana had eaten at one of the colonial taverns made famous by visits from General Washington.

What was the name of the place? Christine's?

Liana had complained the whole meal because the food was colonial fare, not her stupid alfalfa sprouts and leaves.

Christina—no, Christiana Campbell's Tavern. A favorite place where General Washington ate seafood. Kirby snapped his finger, the sound lost in the ringing in his ears. Wind blew down the neck of his shirt and he shivered.

His ancestors hunkered down in their coats as the wind chilled them too. Étienne's face grew even more solemn, the gaunt hollows in his cheeks more noticeable in the gaslight. He raised his hands, removed the emerald ring from his left hand and placed it in his son's palm. Louis shook his head and thrust his hand toward his father. Etienne folded his fingers over his son's and pushed their joined hands to Louis' chest.

Finally, the younger man accepted and slipped the ring over his finger. Étienne smiled and clasped his son's shoulder in the same way the general had.

Kirby's ring throbbed on his own finger. He glanced down. The stone glowed, an electrifying sparkle of green light that pulsed as it brightened and dimmed.

He made eye contact with Louis at the same time as the magnetic pull that would take him to another dimension seeped into his skin. His feet remained rooted in place as his upper body extended until he thought he would break. Like a rubber band stretched too tight, his body snapped. His feet lifted from the step, and he shot into the spinning wormhole.

CHAPTER 18

"Does Anybody Really Know What Time It Is?"

5th Toll of Midnight
Portsmouth, Virginia Present Day

The parlor clock struck midnight, the echoing peal muffled by the closed bedroom door. Sandi peeked into the bedroom. Norrie still slept, curled up with Maggie the doll.

Sandi turned back to wash her hands at the sink, then splashed cold water over her face. Her nerves had settled, and she thought about making a cup of chamomile tea to help her get back to sleep.

Muffled sobs started, intensity increasing and fading. Sandi burst from the bathroom, determined to find the source of the mysterious weeping. Her gaze shifted from the open bedroom door to the bed.

Norrie was gone.

"Mommy?" The childish voice gurgled, as if underwater.

"Norrie!" Sandi yelled and raced out the door, skidding on a runner lining the hallway.

The clock struck again, the clang more urgent and pronounced. Sandi crashed into a small end table as she rounded the corner of the wall and entered the parlor.

A green glow from the mirror cast the room in shimmering waves of light and shadows. Sandi could make out Norrie's small form, doll clutched to her chest as she stepped toward the fireplace.

"Stop!" The clock struck thrice, the gong reverberating and drowning Sandi's shout. She vaulted over the table and scooped her child in one arm. Norrie threw one arm around her mother's neck, the other pressed between their chests as Sandi hitched her daughter's legs around her waist. The clock and bric-a-brac on the mantle rattled. Sandi caught her reflection in the mirror. Green light enveloped the image of her holding Norrie, their shapes distorted by undulating reflections.

On the fifth clang of the clock, a rush of air blew from the glass, whipping the woman and child's hair into stinging nettles that lashed their faces. The room rattled with the thunderous winds, as if a freight train headed straight at them.

Norrie screamed and burrowed her head further into Sandi's shoulder.

"Clasp your feet together behind me, baby," Sandi shouted above the roar. "Hold on." The hard plastic of the doll's arm dug into her ribcage as she pressed her daughter closer. Sandi planted one foot in front of the other and braced against the wind to keep from being blown over.

A moment of absolute silence filled the air, followed by the clock tolling another bell of the hour.

As suddenly as it began, the wind reversed, spinning Sandi and her daughter counter clockwise. Sandi's hair thrashed her other cheek, and she angled her body to shield Norrie from the new assault as they spun.

The dim glow burst into jagged green flashes as the winds sucked back into the mirror, pulling Sandi and Norrie into the murky infinity behind the quicksilver.

Kirby
Portsmouth, Virginia 1781

Kirby spun and skidded along the grass, landing between two bushes near a wooden bench. Branches scratched at his face and arms, but the welcome heat of summer greeted him, and he basked in the brilliant sunlight.

"This is ridiculous," he muttered as he pulled twigs and leaves from under his collar and moved into a kneeling position.

Horses clopped by, wagons rattling behind them. Children laughed as adults called to each other.

I can hear!

Eyes raised to the sky in gratitude, Kirby let the sounds of normal life filter through his brain. He pushed aside the branches and peered through the slats of the bench. He was in a farmer's market of some sort. Baskets of produce were stacked high on tables encased in stalls, or on other tables in the open. A weathered man in white shirt and tan leather breeches stood on the far side of the market square. Two baby calves grazed nearby, tethered to a peg attached to a stand laden with vegetables.

Men and women strolled past, stopping at stalls here and there.

Two soldiers walked near the bench, chatting with merchants before stopping inches from Kirby's location. The second soldier faced Kirby's bench and with a subtle movement removed his pocket watch. He snapped the cover shut after a quick glance.

"We can wait no longer, Louis," he whispered. "Perhaps they cannot make it to Market Square as agreed."

Louis! Kirby's eyes were level with the backs of the second soldier's knees, white-trousers tucked into high black boots.

"They arrive as we speak, James." Louis's voice rang with relief.

Kirby hunched lower behind the bench. He wasn't taking any chances. So far, he had been invisible to the occupants of this colonial world he had entered, only seeming to be noticed by a juvenile Louis as Kirby was about to depart.

Squinting between two slats, he observed two teenage girls walking briskly across the square, with a much younger child between them. The tallest girl, brown-haired and solemn, carried an empty wicker basket in the crook of one arm. The other young lady with reddish-gold hair and a smattering of freckles across her nose carried a basket covered with a checkered linen cloth.

The sisters had grown into pretty young women since he

had last seen them. Theresé looked to be about seventeen, the other slightly younger. Marie Josephé's free hand clutched that of the littlest girl, who skipped beside her to keep up with her sisters' strides. Under her arm, the child clutched a doll wrapped in the same red checkered pattern as the cloth covering the basket.

The little girl broke free of her sisters' hands and skipped to the two soldiers.

"Hello. My sisters baked some treats for the English soldiers," she said. "Would you like one? Marie Josephé says it is nice to do something for the soldiers who are far away from their families."

The soldier named James smiled at the girl.

Marie Josephé thrust the basket toward Louis. "Our goods numbered ten and five Dutch cakes but we ran afoul of two of your men. They detained us and uninvited, they each took three cakes from my basket. We still have an even dozen apple tarts left to sell to the sailors."

Louis nodded and took the basket. "I apologize for the boorish behavior of my fellow soldiers."

"They should be drawn and quartered," Marie Josephé mumbled. Theresé elbowed her in the side.

Nicole thrust her doll out in a move nearly identical to Theresé's in the family Christmas scene Kirby had witnessed earlier. He recognized the same doll, although older and more worn. The child smiled at James and said, "My name is Nicole. Who are you? Do you like my baby?"

The older sisters stiffened. Theresé straightened her spine, while the redheaded Marie Josephé's knuckles turned white as they tightened around the handle of the basket.

Louis stepped forward. "May I introduce myself, ladies? I am Captain Lawrence, and this is my most trusted solider, Corporal James Beecher." Both older girls relaxed.

Captain Lawrence! Kirby shifted to a more-comfortable kneeling position as he studied the scene unfolding before him. He had no concept of time anymore. Louis still stood with his back to him, and Kirby recalled his previous time travel episode with his ancestors meeting General Washington. He remembered Kyle's accounting of Louis as an American spy in the British Army, so he assumed the general had tasked the young man with a mission.

Are they talking in code? Fifteen of something Dutch. Another twelve of something else. Dutch what? Ships? Weapons?

Why didn't I cover this in my research paper?

The littlest girl turned her attention to Louis, tugging the hem of his coat and motioning him toward her. Louis knelt in front of her. She clutched the doll to her chest as if to protect it, then held it under his nose. "Do you like my baby?"

Louis nodded. "She is very pretty."

"The step-grandmama took it from me and said it was old and ugly." The toddler pouted. "She threw it in the bin. My sisters got it out for me and even sewed a new dress."

Louis took the doll and held it close to the child's head. "She is most lovely, as are you." When the little girl giggled and turned her head to look up at her sisters, Louis ran his fingers near the skirt, withdrawing a tiny paper scroll from the hem and replacing it with another. If Kirby had not been viewing from the angle near the ground, he doubted he would have noticed the deft movement.

Louis rose, and the youngster stretched her hands for the doll. He bent forward and kissed her nose as he returned the doll. She giggled again.

Kirby shifted to take pressure off his weaker leg. *Therese certainly resembles Terry.* The colonial girl possessed the same strength and confidence as her many-great granddaughter exuded in modern time.

Theresé spoke. "Nicole, you walked very fast to keep up with us. Would you like to sit on the bench and rest with your baby while Marie Josephé and I talk to the soldiers for a minute more?"

"Yes, please." Nicole backed to the bench and wiggled until she was seated. She cradled the doll in her arms, crooning softly. Theresé took Louis' elbow and Marie Josephé slipped her hand in the crook of the other. They strolled a few feet away and spoke quietly.

To Kirby, and he assumed to passersby, Louis and James appeared to be two flirtatious soldiers engaging pretty girls in animated conversation.

"Why are you sitting in the bushes?" Kirby gave a start at the voice and rolled his eyes upward. Nicole knelt backwards on the bench and peered at him with startling blue eyes.

The kids. It's always the kids who can see.

"I dropped..." Kirby racked his brain for a plausible item. His gaze dropped to an old metal button underneath the bench. "I dropped my button and there it is." He reached for the metal encased in dirt.

"Do you like my baby?" Nicole's attention had already moved on. As she had done with the soldiers, she poked the doll close to his face. Although the face had different paint, and the yarn hair was long gone, Kirby recognized the doll as the beloved Christmas gift the toddler Therese had received.

"What? Oh, yes, she's nice." He slipped the button into his pocket.

"What's your name?"

"Kirby. And you are Nicole, right?"

"Yes. How do you know my name?"

"I heard your sister call you."

"Oh." Nicolle narrowed her eyes. "You look just like that other soldier, but older. Are you his brother?" Nicole pointed her index finger over her shoulder towards Louis.

Before Kirby could answer, Marie Theresé called, "Nicole, what are you doing?"

Kirby pressed his fingers to his lips. Nicole nodded and mimicked the gesture. A dimple appeared when she grinned.

She turned her face toward her sister. "Just looking." Her voice dropped to a whisper. "Goodbye." Nicole scrambled from the bench and skipped over to stand between her sisters.

Somewhere in the distance, a church bell tolled. Louis peered over Theresé's shoulder and stared right at Kirby. Frowning, he skirted around his sister and strode toward the bench.

Kirby peered between the bench slats and froze when he made eye contact with the solider.

The two men glared at each other. Kirby's jaw dropped. The man in the red coat was not just his spitting image.

He was the image from the mirror.

The tightening in his skin warned Kirby what was to come.

Now I understand how a seismograph detects earthquakes before they start.

He would be gone before Louis reached the bench.

CHAPTER 19

"Time to Say Goodbye"

6th Toll of Midnight
Portsmouth, Virginia 1781

Kirby landed on his hands and knees in mud. Stinging drops of rain pelted his face. The muck made a sucking sound as he lifted himself into a sitting position and surveyed his surroundings.

Nearby, a carriage with restless horses waited. As a flash of lightning lit up the area, the driver's face took on eerie shadows and a child screamed. Kirby recognized Nicole and her sisters in the brief flash of light. The little girl screamed again when a second bolt of lightning followed and struck a nearby tree.

"Quiet, little one." An older man tried to calm her as he settled her in the wagon before he took the small satchels from the two older girls.

"My baby, my baby!" Nicole tried to climb out. The sister Kirby recognized as Marie Josephé gently pushed her sister back into the wagon, not noticing the small red velvet pouch slip from her sleeve and fall to the ground. She stepped on it as she climbed into the wagon, pushing it deep into the mud. As

Theresé clambered in behind her, she too stepped on it and pushed the bag even further into the earth.

"No, child, you must stay in the cart." The man grabbed Nicole as she clambered over the side again while shouting, "My baby, my baby!"

"We will find it later. You must go now."

A third woman clutched the arm of the older man but before she could climb into the wagon, three British soldiers ran into the yard, pointing weapons while shouting, "Halt!"

Without provocation, two soldiers fired, striking both the man and woman. As they fell to the ground, the girls screamed from the wagon. Kirby was stunned when the third soldier raised his rifle at his two comrades and fired, stopping them dead in their tracks. Still holding his rifle, he stepped over them and ran to the wagon.

"Mama!" Marie Josephé scrambled to get out of the wagon.

"Go, go!" the soldier urged. Kirby realized it was Louis. "There is no time now. I couldn't stop the soldiers in time. I will take care of mother and grandfather, but you must go. Father will be waiting for you at the camp. Tell him I will get word to him about Mama and Grandfather. GO!"

"Oh, Louis." Marie Josephé hugged her brother and scrambled into the carriage with her sisters, who were huddling together under a canvas cover. The driver whipped the horses into a gallop.

Moments later, three more soldiers ran to the area. Louis shouted for them to look for two men in black cloaks, sending two in the opposite direction of the wagon's path. One soldier remained at his side.

"James!" Louis whispered hoarsely. "It is my mother and grandfather. Help me get them inside." He cradled his mother in his arms while James tended to the unconscious man. The man and woman bled profusely. Three other soldiers ran into the yard, guns drawn, asking what happened.

"There was an ambush. Two soldiers as well as these people were wounded. Some of my men are chasing after them now. Can you find the doctor?"

"Yes, he lives not far from here. I will get him." One of the men holstered his gun and ran back the way he came.

"We need to get these people inside!" Louis shouted. He gathered his mother into his arms and carried her inside, while the men helped James carry Phillip.

Kirby followed behind Louis. The dim lanterns cast shadows on the woman's pallid face. Her head lolled back, eyes closed. Drops of blood splattered on each step. Louis stumbled in the narrow stairwell and again as he reached the landing. Kirby pushed his hands forward, his fingers folding into the cold wet wool of Louis' redcoat. Louis steadied but did not look back. He set Clothiste on the bed. Blood seeped from her left shoulder, staining her dress. Louis ripped linen from a pillow, wadded it and pressed it to the wound.

He whispered, "Mother?"

"Phillip? Is he...?" Clothiste clutched the lapel on Louis's jacket with her good hand.

"They have him in the next room. The doctor is coming."

"The girls—are they safe?"

"They got away, Mother. They will be safe in the camp in a few hours."

"I'm dying, Louis," she whispered.

"Don't say that. You must not talk, mother."

"I love you, my son, and I am so proud of you."

"Please, Mother..." Louis could say no more, as the door burst open and a man with a medicine bag rushed in, followed by a woman with a pan of water. The doctor knelt beside Clothiste and began checking the wounded area. He glanced toward Louis. "You can leave now, soldier," he said curtly and turned back to his patient.

Louis took a step back. A blanched look washed over his face. He moved one step closer to the window, where Nicole's doll rested. The doctor raised his head, one eyebrow raised. Louis turned on his heel and left the room.

Shouts arose below. Kirby stood in the hall. He could see shadows on the stairs.

"Who are you? Look at all this muck and mud," a high-pitched voice cried. "I demand to know what is going on in my home!"

"British soldier, madam," Louis answered. "We brought the gentleman and lady inside. They were accosted by robbers and were both shot."

"Who was shot? Is my husband here? Lizzie, see this soldier out and then come upstairs immediately!"

"Yes, missus."

The older woman thundered up the stairs. She shook rain from her cloak and tossed it to a corner of the hallway. She stopped in front of the room where Clothiste had been taken.

"Where is my husband?" she called.

"In here, Abigail," a voice called from the other room. The woman scrambled into the other bedroom.

Kirby glanced inside the room Abigail had entered.

Like the other bedroom, this one resembled an operating room in an army camp. Muddy footsteps marred the pristine wood floors; bloody strips of cloth littered the areas around the beds; small bed tables were shoved against the wall to make space for the doctors attending the two victims in separate rooms.

In the larger room, Abigail knelt at Phillip's bedside. He was on his stomach, and she took his limp hand in hers as the doctor rattled instruments spread out on the bed beside the stricken man. He groaned, so he was still alive.

Louis' friend James stood near Phillip's shoulder.

"Lizzie!"

"Yes, missus." A young woman in the plain clothes of a servant raced to the door.

"Bring the other doctor in here," Abigail demanded.

"But he is tending to Madam Clothiste," Lizzie sputtered.

"Get him in here," Abigail shrieked, eyes frenzied. Lizzie skittered out of the room, and shortly after, the doctor and the woman helping him both entered the bedroom.

"Mrs. Roker, I am tending to…"

"To hell with her. Help him!" Abigail's face was livid. The doctor joined the other men at Phillip's bedside.

Kirby stiffened with rage at the doctor's decision to leave the patient he was attending. He scrambled back to the other bedroom. The frail woman lay motionless, and he wondered if she was already dead. He reached for her wrist, finding her weak pulse.

Her dress was ripped where the doctor had tended to the wound to her shoulder. Kirby grimaced at the scene. A tenaculum—a kind of forceps consisting of a slender sharp-pointed hook attached to a handle and used mainly in surgery for seizing and holding parts such as blood vessels—had fallen to the floor, crusted with old dried blood and spattered with fresh blood.

Bloody wads of cotton littered the floor, a scalpel lay unprotected on the table beside a flattened piece of lead. The doctor had removed the bullet and placed an herbal poultice over the wound, held in place with a patch of linen. He had not completely bandaged it before going to the other room.

Concerned, Kirby knelt by the injured woman. He had studied the history of medicine during the Revolutionary War. Colonial doctors, unaware of bacteria and the concept of sterilization, did not practice the sanitary hygiene of modern medicine. Bullets were removed only if within easy reach of the surgeon. Often, if a wound had to be closed, a piece of onion was placed in the cavity before closure, and the wound reopened a few days later. Doctors back then considered the development of pus as a sign that the wound was healing.

Kirby leaned forward and caught the unmistakable odor of onion mingled with the pungent herbs. He dug through the contents of a satchel at the bedside. Two small knives, a hacksaw, swatches of loose cotton cloth—some clean, some not—littered the bottom of the leather bag. He scratched his finger on the point of a needle plunged into a spool of thread, a dark strand dangling from the eye. He removed it from the bag, pulled the needle free of the twisted thread, and lined the sewing instruments on the side table.

He pulled out several brown bottles and smelled each, unsure of the contents. He rummaged again until his fingers touched a small flask. He pulled the cork and smelled again.

Whiskey! He grabbed the grimy scalpel from the nightstand and held it over the flickering candle. Gingerly, he pulled the cloth patch away from Clothiste's shoulder and peeled back the small herbal mass over the wound. Skin puckered from the ragged stitches drawn too tightly over the incision. He clipped the stitches and removed the sliver of onion. He poured whiskey on the cleanest of the dubious cloths and dabbed the wound. Next, he threaded the needle and held the point over the flame. He ran the whiskey-soaked cotton down the length of the thread, and with a few flicks of his wrist, he stitched the wound closed.

Without warning, Clothiste's eyes fluttered open. In wide-eyed terror, she tried to contain a fit of coughing. The gasping, wheezing sounds deep in her lungs signaled the consumption Kirby had suspected from her earlier coughing episode back at the camp. He eased her head forward and settled the pillow under her back, mindful of the wound he had just sutured. She looked into his eyes. She tried to speak through parched lips and he moved closer to hear her whisper, "I've been waiting for you. I knew you would come."

Kirby froze in place. *She can see me?* The hairs on the back of his neck rose, sending shivers down his spine as he stared down at his seventh great-grandmother. Her beautiful face was etched with pain, but she managed a weak smile. "You are so like my son. Find him. He will need you."

She groaned and closed her eyes.

The woman servant burst into the room and rushed to kneel at Clothiste's side. She took the injured woman's hand in hers. "Madame Clothiste, can you hear me?" she gasped, tears flowing. She tilted her head and pressed her ear to Clothiste's chest.

"Oh, thank God, you are alive."

Clothiste mumbled something that Kirby could not hear. The servant looked in his direction, and her eyes widened in fear. She rushed around the bed, and Kirby stiffened, thinking she was about to attack him.

But she passed right by him without a glance in his direction, and Kirby realized she was not looking at him. Instead, she ran to the window seat and grabbed the small figure. She lifted the doll's skirt and removed a small scroll of paper. Dropping to her knees in front of the bench, she pressed a panel in the wall. A secret door opened. The maid propped herself up as she reached far inside, tucking the doll into a corner behind the alcove wall.

She closed the panel, scrambled to her feet and raced back to Clothiste's side.

A church bell tolled far in the distance, and Kirby prepared himself. A knifelike pain stabbed through the top of his skull and shot down to his feet as the winds roared around him, drowning out the bell's clanging echo.

CHAPTER 20

"Midnight Visitor"

7th toll of Midnight
Portsmouth, Virginia Present Day

Distant crying woke Stephanie. She sat bolt upright in her bed and looked around. Gage was at work. Only silence greeted her ears now as she listened in the darkness.

It must have been a dream. She had fallen asleep reading some of the old family letters, with Clothiste's Inn on her mind. The communiqué about the missing child had haunted her since she'd discovered it. She reached for the table light. The blankets shifted, rustling papers she had fallen asleep reading.

This was a new stack of correspondence from an antique leather satchel she discovered in the attic of the inn. Stephanie had begun the arduous task of cataloguing hundreds of pieces of family correspondence Gage's mother had collected over the years. A jumble of mixed kinfolk writings, these stacks were in no particular order, therefore she had to peruse each piece in order to place it in the correct sequence. She created columns designating the date of the missive, the sender, the recipient, and a brief synopsis of the contents.

She propped against the headboard and grabbed a stack of letters, hoping to find one that would shed more details on the little girl Maggie's disappearance.

Apprehension washed over her. She shivered and rubbed her arms as if to ward off the unease.

Something was wrong, but she could not put her finger on it. Her teardrop-shaped diamond necklace warmed on her skin, a sensation she had not experienced since the night they had dedicated the opening of Clothiste's Inn.

Something's wrong at the inn. I've got to check on Sandi. *She reached for her phone and scrolled until she located Sandi's number. She pressed her fingers to her mouth at the first ring of the phone.* What am I going to tell her?

The ringtone changed after the pause. The second sound tolled more like a bell in her ear than the normal ringing. She held the phone away from her head as the third gong pierced the silent room. When Sandi's answering machine failed to kick in and the tolling became unbearable, Stephanie clicked on the end call button.

Unexplained but convincing cold chills ran down her spine. Something was definitely wrong at Clothiste's Inn.

She punched in the number for Terry first. She would follow with a call to Mary Jo.

Kirby
Portsmouth, Virginia 1781

Kirby shot through an invisible barrier and skidded on his knees, scraping his shins on sharp brick steps as his head struck the side railing of a small porch. He glanced around. An alley separated the property from another home across the back yards. By his surroundings, he surmised that he had landed on the back steps of a fairly large house. A spindly magnolia tree stood in the right rear corner of the yard, not far from a small outbuilding. Closer to the main house, a clothesline sagged under the weight of men's clothes. Several pairs of tan breeches and two white shirts hung motionless in the heat, ends touching the ground. The support pole was already tilted too far to raise the rope higher.

A woman's angry voice drifted from a window at his left. Kirby rolled from the steps to a bush directly under the window. Branches scratched his face and arms. Oppressive summer heat sent beads of sweat along his forehead. His ears popped as if he had dropped from a high altitude.

This time travel shit is getting damn hazardous to my health. Kirby shook his head and swallowed hard to clear his ears.

"You careless snit." A high-pitched woman's voice repeated the insult, followed by a resounding slap.

A small child cried out in pain.

The woman's voice lowered. Kirby could not make out the words, but another sharp slap followed. This time the child did not make a sound.

"Get out now and finish this laundry or you will be thrashed to within an inch of your life."

The wooden door burst open. Kirby peered through the porch railings. A tiny pair of feet, encased in shoes that were far too large, stepped onto the brick. The girl dragged a wicker basket full of laundry by one handle, the other end bumping each step as she progressed to the bottom step and into the yard. Straining in a backward walk, she hauled the wicker basket with her. Once, she heaved too hard and lost her balance, the container landing on her ill-fitting shoes and pinning her feet in place.

The child struggled to free her shoe tips, then continued across the yard toward the smaller rear outbuilding. She crossed the threshold and turned her back to the door, hauling the basket over the step. The momentum propelled her onto her behind. With a final tug on the handle, the girl scooted backward and dragged the laundry basket over the doorsill. The door slammed behind her.

The sun beat right on the spot where Kirby hid, as if a wayward kid held a magnifying glass over a squirming insect. Sweat trickled down his spine. *Freaking heat.* He held his hand to the sky to block the searing glare, expecting the move to prove fruitless. He was solid as a rock. Perspiration beaded on his forehead, and he swiped it with the back of his hand. *If no one can see me, or hear me, how is it I can see and feel everything around me?*

After a quick glance at his surroundings, Kirby scuttled from his hunched position and streaked across the grass to the water pump. He worked the handle until a gush of water ran out. He cupped his hands and took two huge gulps before swiping water over his head. Darting across the grass, he snatched a shirt and pair of breeches from the line to replace his tattered clothes. The door to the smaller building snapped open. He dove headfirst into a line of bushes and rolled to a crouched position. He had a clear view of the rear of the main house and could see the front of the smaller building if he risked poking his head around the corner.

The girl dragged the basket again, this time down the steps toward the clothesline. Her loose-fitting shoes slapped the ground as she struggled to toss the sheets over the line, grunting with the effort. She managed to spread the linens on the sagging line, the ends dipping dangerously close to the dirt. She carried the empty basket back to the house. She spoke to someone inside, her childish voice rising in anguish. A soft female voice soothed the young girl, but Kirby could not make out the words.

A moment later the little girl skittered outside and ran to the sagging clothesline. With a grunt and a mighty heave, she struggled to lift the support pole, raising the clotheslines a mere few inches. She looked from side to side in desperation, and her gaze settled on Kirby. He sank lower behind the tiny tree.

"Who are you? Why do you wear those funny clothes?" she asked, looking right into his eyes.

"You can see me?" Kirby raised his head in surprise, then ducked low again, tucking the just-pilfered colonial clothes behind him.

"Of course I can. You are right there."

What was the old saying? Out of the mouths of babes? Kirby said the first thing that came to mind. "I am playing a game."

"Oh, hide and seek?" The little girl's face grew wistful. "I used to play hide and seek with my brothers, but I got lost-ed sometimes and they would get mad. I've been waiting for you. Will you take me home after I finish my work?" She turned her attention back to the support pole, wet laundry dragging the ground. She struggled with the awkward post for another full minute. Kirby started to rise from his position to help the child when a red-sleeved arm thrust one of the sheets aside. Kirby crouched and lowered his head. He shrugged out of his 21st-century clothes, shrugging into the shirt and breeches he had pilfered.

"What have we here, a damsel in distress?" A British soldier stepped between the drooping linens, his back to Kirby. He spoke in a jovial voice as he offered to help the child. The thin girl angled her head to look at Kirby. With a shake of his head, he touched his finger to his lips.

The soldier lifted the pole and tucked the rope into the wedge cut out of one end. With a single heave, he raised it until the sheets hung clear and he lodged the pole in the dirt. The bed linens flapped in the breeze, shielding his redcoat from the main house.

He whistled once, low and sharp, and stepped closer to the small building Kirby crouched beside. The British soldier flicked his wrist in the direction of the shed. A round object whizzed by and landed with a thud inside the door.

Was that a paper note wrapped around a rock?

Kirby craned his neck as far as he dared.

A low, weak chirp answered from inside.

The soldier nodded and pursed his lips. He gave two short tweets, then knelt beside the girl and asked, "What's your name, little one?"

"My name is Margaret." She stroked the soldier's cheek.

"I'm Louis."

"Lou-wee," Margaret drew out the syllables. In spite of the soldier's English pronunciation, she repeated the name with a decidedly French accent.

Just like Tanner and Norrie had done, Kirby remembered. Hackles danced along his collar and he hunkered lower.

"Can you keep a secret, Miss Margaret?" Louis inclined his head toward the child in a conspiratorial manner.

"Yes." She touched her forehead to his and giggled. "My brothers keep secrets from me all the time. Now I can have one too."

"Should anyone ask you if you have seen a soldier just now, you must tell them no. Do you understand?"

"Even Miss Lizzie?"

Louis glanced toward the outer house. "Miss Lizzie knows I'm here. But no one else must find out. Promise?" He narrowed his eyes, his roaming gaze settling on the bushes.

Kirby shrunk lower, praying the shrubs hid him from view.

"I promise." Margaret crossed her heart and kissed Louis' cheek.

Louis stood up and looked straight into Kirby's eyes. As he strode toward the shrubs with purposeful strides, his scabbard slapped his thigh.

The distant gong of a clock rebounded into a series of echoes that pierced Kirby's eardrums. The vortex pulled him into its grip, pain searing his body as if his limbs were being shredded.

He disappeared into another dark crevice of time.

CHAPTER 21

"It's Not My Time"

8th Toll of Midnight
Portsmouth, Virginia 1781

The ragged streak of lightning illuminated Kirby's surroundings and revealed he had arrived at the outdoor kitchen again, his back smashed against the side of the small building. The rumble that followed indicated the rains would soon begin. To his left, the kitchen door opened on a squeaky hinge.

"Louis?" a woman whispered.

"Lizzie?" The man's voice rasped, his footsteps squishing in the mud until he reached the crunch of the broken seashells surrounding the steps.

"Here, Louis." In the illumination of the next lightning strike, Kirby saw the outline of the servant girl leaping into the red-coated arms of Louis. The little girl Margaret stood in the doorway.

Louis broke the embrace on a clap of thunder. "You must come now."

"I have to take the child with me, Louis."

"'Tis not room enough, Lizzie."

"I will share my space with her. Louis, please, I cannot leave her behind. I have prepared her, she knows that whatever happens, she must remain still and quiet."

Louis scooped Margaret in his left arm and said, "Lizzie, take my sleeve. We must leave now." He pressed his scabbard against his thigh and led Lizzie to the left of the big house.

Kirby scrambled to follow as they ran toward a churchyard where a wagon waited, the impatient horse whinnying and lurching forward. A man grabbed the horse's bridle, stroking its muzzle until the animal settled. Kirby shrunk behind a tree, then wondered why he needed to hide if children were the only ones who could see him.

"Climb in the front seat with James, Lizzie," Louis ordered. "I will settle the child in the back, under the canvas."

"I will be good." Margaret wrapped her arms around Louis' neck and pressed her cheek against his.

He squeezed her thin shoulders and thrust her over the side. "This corner has some space where you can curl. Goodbye, little one."

"Are you not coming?" Lizzie reached for Louis' arm.

"Not yet. James is deserting the King's service tonight. I shall remain for a while to distract."

James clambered into the seat and picked up the reins.

Louis extended his arm and the men shook hands.

"Be safe, my love." Lizzie leaned down and pressed her lips to his.

Louis tucked a canvas cover over Lizzie's legs and said, "I shall follow soon. I must see my grandfather before I leave." He stepped back and swatted the horse's flank. A vivid streak of lightning electrified the night sky. Thunder boomed, warning that the storm rolled ever closer.

The wagon veered, and Kirby jumped from its path. The bulky wagon lumbered forward, swallowed by the night shadows.

Louis pivoted and ran in the direction from which they had just come, Kirby on his heels. Louis darted down the street and scurried between houses into an alley. A bolt of lightning revealed they had reached the back of the same outdoor building. Louis strode forward. Kirby pressed his back to the house and peered around the corner. Louis had reached the steps of the main house. Kirby moved in closer. Lightning illuminated Louis' figure, the red coat a shocking contrast to the lack of color in the night gloom. He rotated a key in the door, pressing his finger against the metal. The simple act muffled the click of the lock. Pushing the door inward, Louis stepped into the silent room, and waited.

Kirby inched closer as Louis lifted a lantern from a hook near the door and set it on the floor. After some shuffling around, he knelt and struck flint until he produced a spark. The tinder flared, and he lit the lantern wick.

The flame forced shadows in the hollows of Louis's gaunt face. Wooden floorboards creaked under his feet as he walked further into the house. He raised the lantern to shine on the floor.

"Mother!" Louis whispered hoarsely and knelt by Clothiste's side. She lay in a huddled heap at the base of the stairs. In the lantern's reflection, her face was colorless, her lips blue. Blood pooled under her injured shoulder and spread down the sleeve of her gown.

She struggled to open her eyes and move her lips. He cupped her neck and tried to raise her head. He bent his ear to her face, her gasp fluttering against his skin. Kirby moved as close as he dared.

"My son." She tried to raise her good arm but could only shift her wrist.

"Don't talk, Mother."

"She tried...to kill...Phillip," Clothiste whispered, voice breaking between gasps of breath. Tears trickled from her half-opened eyes, sliding along her temples to the floor.

Her jaw slackened. A gurgle rattled deep in her throat. Louis gathered his mother's limp form, muffling sobs against her neck.

Weak groans emitted from above, near the stairs. Kirby

could make out a form at the top of the steps. He struggled to recall the story Stephanie had told him, of the battle Clothiste had had with her step mother-in-law that led to their deaths. They called her "The Wicked One" but what was her real name? *Abigail?*

"Who is down there? Help me." Abigail's weak yet petulant voice called.

Louis gently lowered his mother's shoulders to the floor. Her blood smeared his right hand, obscuring the emerald of the signet ring on his finger.

Kirby's ring burned against his own skin.

"Who is there?" The raspy voice above groaned again.

"British soldier." Louis brushed his mother's cheek with his clean hand and stood up. He held the lantern higher and began a deliberate ascent. Floorboards creaked as he knelt beside Abigail.

"Never mind the whore at the bottom of the steps." the woman upstairs said. "Do you know who I am?" She shifted and screamed in pain. "Do your duty."

Kirby rushed to Clothiste's limp body, pressing fingers to her throat. After a few seconds, a trace of weak pulse moved under his skin. Clothiste groaned, then inhaled a jagged breath. Lightning flashed and illuminated her death mask. She looked at Kirby. He bent closer to hear as she whispered, "I've been waiting for you. Help him. Help my son." The words ended with a gurgle as she exhaled her final breath.

Delayed thunder rumbled. The storm moved away.

He turned his eyes to the top of the stairs where Louis knelt beside a sprawled woman. Louis jumped to his feet and disappeared into a room. The murmur of male voices drifted to Kirby's ears. Gaze locked on the top step, he moved to the side of the other woman.

Her head rested on the floor, her body aiming downward. One leg stretched before her. The other twisted at an odd angle, the heel almost reaching her hip. As he had done previously, he checked for a pulse.

As before, his fingertips detected the weak beat of a dying

heart. Lightning lit up the hall through a small window and he glanced into Abigail's face, twisted and distorted in the shadows.

Lantern light shifted as Louis emerged from the middle room and entered another doorway. As he reentered the hall, he stopped short and knelt beside Abigail. He leaned back on his heels, staring down at his hands.

The acrid odor of the burning lantern oil wafted to Kirby's nostrils and he coughed.

Louis raised the lantern and turned. The light cast flickering shadows under his chin. He raised his other hand to Kirby and pleaded, "Help me. Dear God, please help me."

Kirby reached for Louis' outstretched hand. A spark of green electricity snapped between the emerald rings adorning their fingers. A clock in the parlor emitted a chime and a split-second later a church bell tolled once.

One o'clock.

Kirby closed his eyes as the room spun around and he flipped into darkness.

CHAPTER 22

"I Just Wasn't Made for These Times"

9th Toll of Midnight
Portsmouth, Virginia 1781

The vortex stopped, dropping the bottom from under Kirby's feet. He shot toward the ground feet first, sinking to his ankles in muck and mud near a spindly tree. His knees buckled from the impact, but he managed to straighten without losing his balance. He recognized he was once again back in the alley behind Louis' grandfather's house.

In his peripheral vision he spotted the outline of a woman. He looked towards her and raised his arm just in time to stop the swing of a board from striking his head. The plank cracked against his forearm and he lowered his injured limb, wincing in pain. With gritted teeth, he shook his head and opened his eyes, turning just in time to see a curled fist looming toward his face.

Incredible pain shot through his head as knuckles crashed, first into his nose, and then his cheek. His vision filled with exploding fireworks until he crumpled to his feet, out cold.

***

A multitude of foul odors invaded Kirby's sense of smell as he regained consciousness. The stench of unwashed bodies and human waste mixed with dank earth, mildew, and the odd sickening-sweet smell of old molasses and sugar. Under his nose, the coppery tang of crusted blood—his blood—filtered through the other smells.

Dingy sunlight crept in through long narrow windows caked with dirt. He squinted, unable to make out where he was. He touched his hand to his face. His right cheek and nose puffed with swelling, his eye on that side nearly closed shut. He carefully rotated his jaw and grimaced from side to side, testing his facial bones.

Painful, but nothing seemed broken.

"Who are you?" A low voice hissed only inches from his left ear. Startled, Kirby turned and with his good eye gazed at Louis.

"Where are we?" Kirby rasped, his throat raw and dry. "What happened? Who punched me in the nose?"

"Keep your voice down. We do not want to draw attention. Who are you and why do I keep seeking you?"

"You're Louis, aren't you? Did you hit me?" Kirby touched his nose again. "I remember now. A girl was swinging a board and I raised my hand to stop it. Then someone else punched me in the face."

"I am afraid it was I who struck you. Who are you?"

Kirby again ignored the question and demanded, "No, you tell me first. Why the hell did you punch me?"

"You grabbed the stick from my sister and I was afraid you were going to use it on her. It was my first instinct." Louis sat upright, with his back against the wall. "And you have been aggravating me my whole life. Since I was a child, I have seen you coming in and out of my existence like a visiting ghost that would disappear. Once at Christmas. Then another time I saw you hiding by a wagon at our camp. I was just a boy, maybe ten, and I looked for you but didn't see you by the cart. I thought you had run into the woods, so I followed. I got lost for hours, separated from my family. I wandered a long way and stumbled into a small camp of British soldiers. They were very kind to me. Finally, my father and his friend found me. The soldiers accepted the story that Papa and Richard were simple farmers. As we were riding away in the wagon I saw you in the back. I shouted for my father to stop the wagon. When we stopped, you were not there. I got into much trouble because of you. Who are you?"

"You would not believe me if I told you." Kirby pulled into a sitting position. Blood pounded through his face, and a fresh flow dripped from the wounded nostril. He blocked it with the top of his fist. "Is this a jail? Are we in Portsmouth?"

Louis nodded. "This was once a sugar warehouse. Benedict Arnold commandeered it as a jail for American soldiers."

"I thought I could smell a lingering odor of molasses or cane sugar, mixed with all the horrible smells. How did we get here?"

"Right after I hit you, some troops converged upon us, thinking we were engaged in a brawl or an attack upon the woman, who is my sister Theresé."

"Why are *you* here then? Are you not an officer in the British Army with them?"

"Aye, that I am. They once suspected me of being a spy—which I am." Louis dropped his voice to a whisper. "James and I knew our identities were close to being uncovered. I got him away with our co-conspirator Lizzie and the little servant girl she rescued. I had to come back to my grandfather's house one last time." Louis clamped his hands over his forehead and dragged them downward to rub his eyes. "Then my sister arrived after…after…"

Anguished shouts from across the room interrupted Louis. "Guard. Water. Please, I need water." Several other men called for water.

A face appeared between the bars of a small opening of a heavy wooden door. "Pipe down, ye scurvy mutts, before I come in there and kick your bloody arses." The guard remained at the door, glaring at the first unfortunate prisoner until the man silenced. Satisfied he would not be besieged with further requests, the guard moved on.

For several seconds, Louis remained mute, listening until the guard's footsteps faded. He leaned closer to Kirby. "We needed to get James safely away, because once it was discovered he was gone he would be immediately confirmed as a deserter. Instead of trying to make my getaway, I decided that I should return to my post. I could perhaps maintain my cover longer if I remained and allowed the British to assume James was the suspected spy. I planned with my sister for her to knock me out, so that it would appear as if I had been accosted. Next thing I knew, you appeared in our midst just as she swung the board. I struck you. Before we could do anything else, soldiers arrived and we were both taken into custody."

Kirby rubbed his arm. "Be glad that she did not make contact with your head. For such a tiny girl she has a powerful swing. And you're no slouch either."

Louis managed a weak grin. "We often sparred as children. Perhaps she used some childhood indiscretion as her inspiration to carry out her dreadful task upon my person." His expression sobered. "You are not of this world. You look like me, but you are not from here."

Kirby shook his head. "You will not believe me, but what you say is true. I am from your world but not from your time. I come from the future. I know a lot about you because I am descended from you. You died in eighteen-sixty, nearly ninety-seven years old. But I think that when you died, you somehow became trapped in time, and you have been existing in a parallel universe or something. Or I am in an alternate reality within a parallel universe." He held up his dirty hand, showing the ring. "It is fortunate that we are covered in dirt and blood, or the miscreants guarding us would have relieved us of our rings. This ring has been passed down through the generations. At one point, the stone separated from the setting, and one of your great-grandsons—my great-great grandfather—mounted the stone in a new gold frame." Kirby moved his hand closer to Louis' and weak sparks arced between the emeralds.

Louis snapped his wrist back and frowned. "'Tis a good thing we are so bloodied and dirty, for I have no doubt these would have been stolen from us. How can the same stone exist on your hand and mine?"

Kirby shrugged. "I can't explain it and I certainly don't understand how we can both be wearing the same stone at the same time, but I think it plays an important role in why I am here. I believe you are stuck somewhere between the walls of time. A mirror that is now in the house once owned by your grandfather is somehow the portal between our worlds. I saw your image trapped behind the glass once."

"How can this be? Were we to talk of such things in open company, we would be jailed more swiftly than we were today. Or perhaps burned as witches."

"My time is more than two hundred and twenty-five years in the future. I studied about the Independence of America on July fourth, seventeen seventy-six, and the years of war that followed. There are some family records that explained how your family was kicked out of Canada and settle in America. Then your father joined the French army to assist the Americans in the war. Your parents had lost everything, so they followed the garrison as they moved south. They are considered heroes in our modern-day family lore."

Louis bobbed his head in agreement. "My father and Comte de Rochambeau were friends before the war. Washington had wanted to attack the British in New York, but the comte was able to convince him that the Continental Army and the French allies should move south to Virginia. My father was part of an advance scouting team and they began marching toward Virginia in July. I was assigned to a unit here under the traitor General Benedict Arnold. Then William Phillips took over, but he died in May and Cornwallis arrived for a while. Cornwallis received conflicting orders from his commanding officer, and he decided to move his base to Yorktown. Because of my grandfather, who was already an established businessman in Portsmouth, I was able to pass and receive information fairly easily. His wife Abigail, a British-born woman and vocal loyalist, unknowingly provided the perfect cover. No one suspected the household was the location of much passing of secret information."

Kirby nodded. "Rochambeau correctly surmised that control of the Chesapeake Bay was crucial to blocking the British efforts to reinforce their army in Yorktown. It would also prevent the British from escaping through that route. The Comte de Grasse and the French Navy arrived and blockaded the Chesapeake Bay."

A prisoner groaned in a corner and rolled over, chains rattling.

"I've never seen such horrid conditions. These men are sick in here, maybe dying."

Louis nodded. "I have never been in here. I will try to do something about it when I am free."

Kirby paused for a moment. Using his index finger, he drew lines in the dirt on the floor. He pointed to the first row of slashes. "Blockading the bay was a strategic decision that paid off. De Grasse's ships were already anchored in the bay when the British fleet arrived. At that time, most of de Grasse's sailors were ashore, leaving the French fleet vulnerable. But instead of attacking, the British moved into 'line ahead' formation, which gave the French time to prepare some of their ships for battle. Eventually, sea and winds changed to the French fleet's favor. They were able to open their lower gun ports while the sea conditions prevented the British from doing so, because their ships were in danger of water entering the holds. The two navies pummeled each other, although the French sustained less damage. After a few days of cat and mouse games on the open waters, de Grasse returned to the Bay, where he found reinforcements from another French fleet already in place. With the Americans and their French allies on the ground, and the fleet blockading the bay, Cornwallis was effectively shut off from all avenues of escape or fortification from the British army and navy."

"So…if you are from the future, then you know the outcome. We will have victory?"

Kirby grinned and nodded. "Cornwallis surrendered to Washington on October seventeen, seventeen eighty-one."

"That is less than a month's time away. Tell me, is it much different, to live in your time?"

"It is. Life is easier in many ways. Water runs through pipes into faucets right in our homes. We have electricity, something like a lightning charge that runs constantly, thanks to the work of the Benjamin Franklin of your time, that provides constant light or heat to our homes at the touch of a switch. We have boxes called refrigerators that can make ice and keep food cold. We have special…" Kirby struggled for a way to describe cell phones, and continued. "Special small boxes people can hold in their hands. They can see and talk to each other, no matter where in the world they are."

"How can that be?"

Kirby lifted one shoulder. "A lot has happened in the past two centuries. Men and women strive to improve the way we live, and constantly invent machines and equipment that makes life easier." He blew his breath and scratched his chin. *How can I explain what airplanes are?* "We have metal coaches with wings that enable them to fly like great birds and take people across the oceans."

"I cannot believe what you tell me." Louis shifted and stared at Kirby with narrowed eyes. "How can such things—such as this flying machine—be possible?"

"We have an expression 'necessity is the mother of invention,'" Kirby replied. "Mankind discovers a need to make life better and invents methods to do so."

"I wish that I could see such inventions. It must be a perfect world in your time."

Kirby shook his head. "Far from it. My time is full of conveniences and inventions beyond belief. But we still have a world of poverty, injustice, diseases. Natural and manmade disasters create havoc. America still fights wars to protect herself and allies around the world. Today England is her staunchest ally."

"That is unbelievable! America and England are friends?" Louis stretched out as best he could among the bodies of prisoners crammed nearby. A rat scuttled across his feet and jumped onto the shoulder of one sleeping man. Louis used the heel of his boot to push the rat away. The animal skittered under the legs of another prisoner.

Kirby crawled around, checking prisoners. Most were emaciated, gaunt and unwashed. Several bore signs of untended injuries. Maggots oozed from a gaping cut on one man's face.

"When I studied history, there were mentions of deplorable conditions of the British prisons holding Americans during the war. Nothing I ever read about compares to what I see here. These men are dying. Something must be done."

Outside, a key clanked against the wooden door. A squeal from rusting hinges pierced the silence as the wooden door swung outward. Several prisoners stirred. The man who had asked for water groaned again and repeated the request. The same guard who had threatened him earlier kicked at the weakened man's hand as he led two uniformed soldiers into the room. The officers stepped over the forms of men sprawled closest to the door, and glanced around, eyes squinting. Their gazes fell on Louis and Kirby.

"Captain Lawrence." One of the men nodded in his direction, a look of distaste crossing his features as he kicked at the feet of a withered form huddled in a fetal position and crossed the room. He then extended his hand to Louis.

"I am Captain Hughes, this is Lieutenant Marks. You are to come with me, sir. I am ordered to bring you to Major General Hartman, with his apologies for your detention. The Major General is grateful that you captured this man who he believes has been working in conjunction with Corporal James Beecher, who deserted this morning."

Louis ignored the outstretched hand and stood on his own, glancing once in Kirby's direction. "I don't understand, Captain."

The officer jutted his chin toward Kirby. "We've been looking for this spy for months. Corporal Beecher has been suspected of passing information to the Americans, and we believe this is the man he gave it to. In fact, Captain, you were once under suspicion yourself, as you fit the description of the collaborator, but it is clear now that was a mistake, and this is the man we want. We have an eyewitness account that he seemed to appear from nowhere and tried to attack a young woman, when you intervened and struck him. My utmost apologies for your unfortunate detention, but in the confusion, the arresting officers thought it best to bring you both here."

"I look forward to seeing him hang from the gallows like the bloody Americans did to John André last year." The lieutenant raised his rifle and aimed it between Kirby's eyes. "In fact, I should like to shoot this bastard myself right now." The burly guard guffawed.

"Lieutenant, you will disengage that weapon immediately," Captain Hughes ordered. "Should anything happen to this man whilst I am with the Major General, I shall hold you personally responsible. Do I make myself clear?"

The lieutenant lowered the weapon, angry eyes still focused on Kirby. "Yes, sir."

Louis turned to Kirby. "I shall explain to the Major General that you are not the person he seeks and return as soon as possible." Captain Louis Lawrence stepped over prisoners and headed to the door.

Captain Hughes said, "And, Lieutenant, I shall be reporting to the Major General the deplorable conditions of this prison. See to it that every man in here receives water and rations today. And send a doctor to tend to these sick men."

"Aye, Captain," the lieutenant responded as they crossed the threshold. "The guard shall tend to these men immediately."

The mangy guard followed the lieutenant, smirking behind his back. At the door, he turned back and pointed across the room to Kirby. Then he raised his finger to his neck and drew a slicing motion across his throat.

Kirby had no doubt that the guard had not the slightest intention of following the captain's orders but would probably return later to give the newest prisoner an introduction to life in the jail—if not death.

Last to go through the doorway, the sentry slammed the heavy wooden door shut, the clank of the metal key reverberating as he turned the lock. He glanced through the bars of the small window.

The space where the American spy had been sitting was now empty.

CHAPTER 23

"Midnight Ferry"

10th Toll of Midnight
Portsmouth, Virginia Present Day

"I'll pick you up in thirty minutes, Stephanie," Terry said, "Then we'll swing by and get Mary Jo. Have you called her yet?"

"I will as soon as I hang up." Without saying goodbye, Stephanie hung up and hit speed-dial.

Mary Jo answered on the first ring. She didn't even say hello first, but said, "What's wrong, Stephanie?" Her voice held an edge of apprehension at the late-night call.

"Nothing yet," Stephanie stammered. "I know this is going to sound crazy, but I've been trying to call Kirby and Sandi and can't get an answer from either one. I just have a feeling in my bones that something is wrong at the inn. I think we need to get there. Terry's coming for me, and if you'll go, we'll come by and get you."

The phone rustled as Mary Jo moved about. "Of course, I'll go. I'm getting dressed now, but why do you think something's wrong?"

"Oh, I don't know, Mary Jo. I must have had a bad dream or something. Sounds of a crying child woke me up. Of course, there was nothing there. Gage is working, and I couldn't go back to sleep. I started

reading more ancestry stuff, trying to find information on that little missing girl, and I can't explain what, but something disturbed me. And then I remembered that new clerk had left on Friday because she said she heard crying in the inn."

"Yeah, in her booze bottle." Mary Jo sighed. "All right, let's just get to the inn. I'll be ready when you get here."

Terry picked up Stephanie, then thirty-minutes later Mary Jo. After a few minutes passing suggestions back and forth, they rode the near-deserted streets in silence. Periodically Stephanie tried calling both Kirby and Sandi, still getting voicemails for a response.

Terry turned into the parking lot of Clothiste's Inn, headlights illuminating Kirby's and Sandi's vehicles, parked side by side.

Security lights burned from the porch and each corner of the house. None of the rear windows had lights on.

"Maybe we should call nine-one-one," Terry suggested.

"For what? To tell them to send a patrol car because one of us has a gut feeling something's wrong?" Mary Jo leaned forward and tapped a shoulder of each friend. "Did it ever occur to you two that maybe Kirby and Sandi are—you know—sleeping? Maybe even together?"

Terry shook her head. "She has Norrie with her tonight. She wouldn't do anything with her child under her roof."

"Well, we are about to find out. Who has the keys?" Stephanie asked.

"I do," Terry and Mary Jo said in unison. The three friends scrambled from Terry's sports car. Their breaths formed vapors as frost nipped at their noses.

"Jeez Louise, it's frigging cold," Mary Jo complained. She jangled the keys under the porch light until she found the one she wanted.

She paused, key poised at the lock. "We've all opened this door to freezing cold, even in the summer, and encountered a paranormal event. I hope the temperature is normal in there now," she whispered. She pushed the door open and stepped inside, Terry and Stephanie on her heels.

Stephanie breathed a sigh of relief and spoke first. "The kitchen temperature is warm. That's a good sign. Let's check the innkeeper's room first." She flipped the light switch in the hallway. The trio moved together and paused at the open door to the innkeeper's suite.

Mary Jo peeked around the corner. "Sandi?" she called softly. She *repeated the name a little louder. She whispered over her shoulder, "The bed is empty but the bathroom door is open and the light is on. Maybe she's in there with Norrie."*

Stephanie slipped past and looked in the bathroom. She shook her head. Her eyes widened and she pointed. "Look, there's her phone on the nightstand. She never goes anywhere without it."

"All right, this is starting to freak me a little," Mary Jo said. She stepped into the hallway and walked toward the stairs, shouting, "Sandi, Kirby, are you up there?" After hearing no response, the three women went upstairs, turning on all lights and searching the rooms.

In the Colonial Room, Kirby's jacket and jeans were folded across the arm of the wing chair, his shoes resting on their sides by the chair legs. The bathroom door stood ajar.

"Kirby's wallet, phone and keys are on the dressing table," Stephanie whispered. She called out his name again, then Sandi's.

A muffled whimper filtered up the stairs. "That's coming from the parlor," Terry said. The women looked at each other and scrambled down the stairs.

Kirby
Portsmouth, Suffolk, and Yorktown 1781

Kirby spiraled through the vortex with less force than earlier episodes. The only effect on his body resulted from the spinning, with none of the distortions he had experienced on other occasions. Flashing lights were present but more subdued, the peal of the bell less pronounced, the reverberations less jarring to his body.

He hit the ground feet-first, running after a wooden wagon with a short, boxed frame on the back.

Louis's face appeared over the backboard. "Hurry!" He motioned frantically. Kirby sped up and stretched his arm. Louis grabbed Kirby's wrist and yanked him into the wagon. He fell with a dull thump into a scrunched sitting position, his head inches from a wood ceiling.

Just outside the forward opening of his cramped space a lantern swayed, casting arcs of light which swayed with the motion of the conveyance in which he had landed. A short canvas drape covered the rear opening above the backboard. A wooden barrel rocked, perilously close to rolling on his shoulder but he threw up a hand and steadied it.

"Your sudden appearances continue to startle me to within one inch of my life," Louis' hoarse voice grumbled in the dark.

Kirby started and bumped his head on the low ceiling. "Yeah, well, they're not doing much for my good health either," he griped. "Where am I now?"

"You arrived just in time. We are approaching a private farm in Suffolk to catch a ferry. We cannot take the Sleepy Hole Ferry because of British forces, but there is a farmer working with the Americans who will transport us across the James River in his private water craft. Hopefully the conditions will be favorable for a rapid journey."

"What happened after you left the jail?"

"I met with my superior officer, convincing him I was unaware of Corporal Beecher's espionage activities. Poor James. If we do not win this war and he is captured, I fear he will be one of the first to be executed. I led the Major General to believe I had captured you as a possible secret agent because you looked so much like me. He sent for you and that was when we received word that you had somehow escaped."

"Well, thank goodness I escaped, or your major general would be having me drawn and quartered as a spy by now."

"I was already thinking our way out of that. I hoped to have a good account devised by the time you were brought to us."

"You seem good at that."

"It is necessary in this war. Thank goodness, I had no need to provide a worthy story. And you have an extraordinary skill with your sudden appearances. How do you do that?"

Kirby lifted one shoulder in a shrug. "Wings. Happens every time a bell rings," he said. Louis glanced at him, one eyebrow raised.

Before Kirby could explain the theory of angels and wings from the old Christmas movie, the driver shouted "Whoa!" and the horses stopped short. Additional voices engaged in conversation with the driver, as footsteps thumped along the wagon sides. The sulfurous odor of pungent marshland drifted in the crisp air. Short waves slapped the shore nearby.

Wood creaked as the backboard was lifted from the slot and the canvas parted. The driver poked his head inside and shined the lantern, his gaze landing on Kirby first. "Where the bloody 'ell did he come from?" the driver bellowed. Another man stood beside him, also holding a swaying lantern.

"It is all right, good sir, he is with me." Louis scrambled from the back. Kirby followed, arms wrapped as the cold air sliced through his thin shirt. Louis continued, "He works with me and was captured. He escaped from the prison and I saw him just as we were starting on our journey. I motioned for him to jump into the wagon. I must deliver him safely to my father. He is very important to Washington and Rochambeau."

"We've tae ge' movin' afore the tides come in," cautioned one of the other men. Dressed in farm clothes, he spoke with a thick Scottish accent. He shook Louis' hand, then Kirby's.

"Mr. McDermott, my father will be forever grateful for the assistance you have provided in the war."

"Mayhap, lad, if the Yankee Doodles can whip the pants off the Brits, 'tis payment enough fer me." He looked at Kirby's thin, dirty shirt. "Lad, ye'll freeze your arse off." He shrugged out of his wool jacket and handed it to Kirby. Ignoring the protests, the Scotsman turned on his heel and walked toward the water.

Kirby slipped his arms through the sleeves and wrapped the wool coat tight. Just enough moonlight graced the sky to illuminate the boat. He cast a dubious glance at the flat-bottom wood vessel. About ten feet wide and maybe thirty feet long, it was little more than a raft, with sides only a few inches high. A ramp at the shore end opened onto the shell-covered wetland. The forms of at least six men sat in the front, holding oars up, waiting. Another man stood with a long pole at the very fore. The wagon driver jumped back to his seat and took the reins. McDermott guided the horses onto the ferry until he was satisfied with their placement, then he wedged triangles of wood under each of the wheels.

He motioned for Louis and Kirby to get into the wagon. "'Tis a long ride ye men have, and water covers the bottom of the boat."

Louis jumped into the rear of the wagon and returned to the corner he had been in earlier. McDermott pulled up the ramp, securing the plank with a hook and pole mechanism. He grabbed a longer pole and pushed the flat craft forward.

Kirby scuttled under the wooden shell and settled in place. "Tell me what happened the day Theresé hit me with the stick. You were covered in blood and dirt. You said your friend James deserted the army."

Louis nodded. He dug through a basket of provisions and removed a flask. He took a long swig and offered the container to Kirby before speaking. "It's best I begin at the beginning. James and I have been friends since childhood. His family and mine have long been close, and they have always sided with the Americans. Our fathers felt we would make good spies for the American army. Washington interviewed me and agreed. I was groomed to infiltrate the British Army and earned my way to positions of authority. James, being of English heritage, enlisted in the army in the regular way, but actually worked with me. We managed to be assigned to Benedict Arnold's forces when they moved into Portsmouth, where my grandfather lived and had many business connections. Mother took seriously ill and Papa feared she was dying. He sent her to his father's house in Portsmouth with my sisters. My grandfather's second wife, Abigail, disliked Mother immediately, and Grandfather soon discovered she was trying to poison Mother. The maid, Lizzie, was Abigail's niece, forced to work as an indentured servant to pay off a debt her mother owed. While working in the household Lizzie found the brown bottle of laudanum."

Cold wind passed over the small craft. Waves slapped against the sides, sending chilling spray over the occupants. One of the men raised the lantern and waved it twice in an arc before returning it to a small niche under the seat. Oars smacked the water as he took up rowing again.

Louis continued. "I also learned that a unit of British soldiers was looking for spies and men were going door-to-door in my grandfather's area. Grandfather arranged for a wagon to take my mother and sisters to Papa's camp, but they were set upon by rogue soldiers and the shootings occurred. The girls got away, but Mother and Grandfather were both shot."

"I saw that event unfold. Your grandfather's name was Phillip, correct?"

Louis nodded. "Lizzie took care of both of them after they were shot, until Abigail dismissed her. She wanted to remain and care for Mother, but Abigail told her our family had already come for her. I knew something was not right, that's why I stayed behind. I wanted to check for myself."

Kirby stretched a kink forming in his neck from the cramped space. Louis shifted as far as he could in an upright position, shoulder leaning against the barrel. He continued, "I ran back to the house and found my mother at the bottom of the steps. She told me Abigail tried to kill my grandfather. Abigail lay sprawled at the top, unable to move. Her legs were horribly twisted. She was near death, I was sure. But I pressed my hands to her windpipe, wanting to hasten her demise." Louis held his hands up. "I have performed magic with these hands, I have drummed signals to troops in battle, I have killed with these hands. Many times in war, I have killed, which does not bother me. But then I murdered Abigail."

Kirby said, "I came to that event too, Louis, but you…"

Louis went on as if Kirby had not spoken. "My grandfather was in his room, barely alive. He knew he would not live through the night. I told him what I had done. He gathered amazing strength and told me I had to bury Abigail under the magnolia tree that had recently been planted. I was to make it appear as if she had killed him and mother, then disappeared. He had several friends who knew Abigail had tried to poison Mother, that she was capable of killing. I was to find Mr. McDermott, to have him go to the house to find my grandfather and mother, so that I could stay clear of trouble. As far as the British Army was concerned, I had no business being at that house. I didn't agree, but Grandfather insisted. After I gave him my word, he died with me at his side."

Through the front opening, light moved as the ferryman lifted the lantern and once again swung it in two wide arcs. He slipped the lamp into the niche. Ten seconds later, he duplicated his actions. At the sound of shouting, the boat drifted to a stop. Louis stopped speaking as more voices joined in. Swaying light washed over the cramped space. Water slapped against the sides while wood creaked as planks rubbed together in time with the rocking.

"Don't say anything," Louis whispered. He strained to listen.

Moments later, one of McDermott's oarsmen appeared at the rear of the wagon and shined the lantern inside. With only his face lighted, he looked like a floating head in the dark. He said, "The scouting team will guide us through the channel to a safe place to disembark. Perhaps another half hour and you will be on your way."

Louis lifted a hand in salute. When the canvas fell back across the opening and the rowing started, he continued.

"As Grandfather instructed, I buried Abigail in the dark, during the storm, and then I hid in the small outdoors building they used as a kitchen in the summer. Troops were out in force once news of James' 'desertion' became known. They would assume I had deserted with him, so I could not just show up before my unit. I had to concoct a story that would satisfactorily explain my absence. I hid there through the entire day, waiting for darkness, the thought of what I had done causing me great anguish. Several times I could hear patrols in the alley behind the kitchen. Then Theresé arrived. I startled her when she slipped into the kitchen looking for the key to the big house. Once I calmed her down, we were able to talk."

"I know a little of this story because Theresé—all of your sisters, in fact—were trapped by the past, each in their own way. Their ghosts appeared to three women at different times and needed help before they could rest."

"And I am not a ghost to you, but a man trapped in time?"

Kirby nodded.

Louis sighed, then continued. "My sister told me that Lizzie had arrived at their camp, where she expected to find Mother, who of course was not there. Father immediately arranged for Theresé to travel back to Portsmouth with old family friends, a Scottish couple with no love lost for Abigail, to find out what happened. She would get help from Mr. McDermott, brother to the man that is helping us now, to take care of our mother and grandfather. But I found her first. She was to strike me to put a few bruises on me and leave me to be found. Everything went according to our plan until you showed up just as she swung the board at me."

"And you knocked my lights out." Kirby touched his face again.

"Purely instinctive, and again, my apologies. And while I have many questions to ask you about your time, I suggest we get some sleep. There will be little rest once we get to the other side and face the journey to Yorktown."

Louis slouched and propped his head against the barrel with his arms across his chest. He soon drifted to sleep. Kirby listened to the slow, steadying breaths of his forefather. He was alive because of this man who lived through the revolution and went on to start a new life and family, fathering the first of a succession of male descendants.

Will the Lawrence line die out with me? The thought echoed in his head. Kirby's own career and relationship with Liana had not left time or room to consider children. And now with their relationship in the tank, he was glad they had never married or had kids.

Sandi came to mind. Kirby stretched out and put his arms behind his head. During all of the incidents with the time travel, he'd barely had time to think about what he was going through, let alone his life in the 21st century. How much time had passed since he had last seen Sandi? On one hand, it seemed like months had passed since they had taken Norrie to

Busch Gardens. But on the other, it only seemed like minutes. Would he ever make it back to Sandi and his time?

He'd like to have a baby with her. The realization struck him with the force of a sledgehammer. It wasn't just for the act of sex, although the pleasant idea sent jolts right to his crotch. She stirred other feelings that he had never experienced before, brought a comfort and peace of mind that he had never known in a relationship—one that he wanted to explore further.

Images of a future with Sandi filled the time until the ferry docked, and the wagon lumbered onto land. Streaks of red sunrise sliced through rips in the canvas covering the back.

Erratic rumbles sounded in the far distance and Louis stirred.

Thoughts of Sandi faded from Kirby's mind as he recognized the strange staccato was not thunder, but cannon fire. The driver shouted, and the horses picked up their pace

"Let us hope that we are not riding into the fray," Louis said. "Have you not slept?"

"No."

"We will be at my father's camp near Yorktown soon, mayhap. You best sleep whilst you have a chance. we know not what awaits us."

Kirby nodded. He doubted he would sleep. Just in case, he rolled his wool jacket under his head and closed his eyes.

***

Explosions roared, still somewhere in the distance but much closer than the earlier ones. The reverberation rippled through the wagon. Kirby jolted upright, trying to gather his wits as he woke from sleep. The wagon no longer swayed with movement. He thrust aside the canvas covering and poked his head outside in time to see Louis carrying a longrifle and disappearing into a wooded area. Two men in civilian clothes followed.

Did I sleep through another time transport or something? Overhead, ominous fall clouds filled the sky. Autumn cold sliced through the thin shirt he wore. He grabbed the jacket he had rolled to use as a pillow. Three more explosions occurred in rapid succession. He scrambled from the wagon, following Louis' path through the copse.

Kirby stopped short at the edge of a clearing. A line of three cannons stretched to his left and two more to his right, manned by men who were fortunately not wearing redcoats. Most wore the blue coats of the French Army, but a few were American soldiers, aided by men in an array of civilian clothes. Other men with muskets and rifles, like Louis, flanked the cannon crews. The bodies of one American soldier and one French soldier lay crumpled at the base of another cannon to the farthest left end of the line.

The artillery aimed across the clearing. Shouts, gunshots, and mortar resounded from that area, where a mounded fortification loomed in the distance. The redoubt from which the British fired was surrounded by a palisade of sharpened tree trunks that provided protection for the occupants inside and created obstacles for the approaching enemy, including ditches and berms that would make an advance on the redoubt more difficult.

Trenches wormed their way on either side as soldiers dug their way towards the redoubt. Lingering smoke swirled as the cannon fire from both sides dissipated across the glade. Acrid vapors reached Kirby's nose, reminiscent of the smell of fireworks and sparklers at 4th of July celebrations. He tried to clear his throat, but a metallic taste lingered. His gaze scoured the field in search of Louis.

The sudden irony struck him that the events he was witnessing were the very reason that Americans were now able to celebrate Independence Day.

Two new soldiers crashed through the thicket, and took up positions at a cannon. The zing of a bullet soared past Kirby's head and he instinctively dropped to a crouch. A heavy weight crashed on his back, knocking him forward. Kirby shifted under the burden that pinned him down and looked into the vacant eye of a soldier. The other eye was gone, along with that half of his face.

Another cannon shot boomed, sending shudders under Kirby's body. Out of the corner of his eye, he could see the howitzer lurch and the plume of smoke billow out of the barrel. A flurry of activity erupted amidst shouts as other mortar shots fired in the area.

A soldier raced through the dissipating smoke and plunged a wet sponge down the barrel. A young boy, no more than ten, scurried from the back of the cannon, carrying a powder charge to the front of the muzzle. He handed it to the first soldier and scrambled to the rear while the soldier rammed the charge down the front of the barrel. The boy returned, staggering under the weight of a cannonball the size of his head. He hefted the ball to the bore just as a gunshot felled the rammer.

Kirby wriggled free of the body pinning him and scrambled to his feet. He raced forward and dropped to his knees beside the newly injured soldier. The massive head trauma revealed the soldier was dead, but Kirby checked for a pulse anyway. A blue blur swished toward him and he angled his head in that direction. A young girl's skirts ruffled the air along his face as she leapt over him and took up the ramrod.

Kirby stared at the willowy girl with auburn hair as she shoved the rod down the barrel.

Mary Jo? No, of course not. She must be Louis' sister.

Marie Josephé stepped back a pace. The gunner primed the weapon and shouted, "*Amorce!*" Kirby's mysterious ability to interpret the French language kicked in, translating the announcement that the weapon was primed. The girl and young boy covered their ears as the gunner lit the powder in the touch hole and yelled, "*Feu.*" The heavy artillery rocked backward with the force of the explosion.

Kirby's fingers didn't reach his ears fast enough to muffle the boom. A high-pitched ringing and internal pressure jolted his auditory senses with a momentary deafness. He shook his head and spat out the sulfuric burn in his mouth as he stood.

The gunner covered the touch hole with the leather thumb

sheath and shouted, "*Prêt.*" Ready. Stepping over the dead soldier, the girl prepared the cannon for the next shot. Kirby tried to remember his American Revolution research paper. *How many "cannon cocker"—cannon crew—did it take to operate a cannon? Three? Five? Nine?* However many it took, the teenage girl and the little boy aiding the lone gunner needed support.

"How can I help?" Kirby shouted. "You are Marie Josephé, right?"

"Yes, I am." She did a double-take. "I know who you are. You look so much like my brother. Please, we need your help." she shouted. She jutted an elbow toward the long-handled wood pole with a cork-screw device at the end. "Push that worm into the barrel and twist it twice to make sure the cannon is clean before we fire the next round."

Kirby followed her directions. Along the ridge, other cannons discharged. Echoing firepower landed far to his left and right, shots returned from unseen British forces hunkered behind the redoubt.

"*Chargez!*" the gunner gave the command to load. The young boy stood ready with the powder charge. As soon as Marie Josephé loaded it and began ramming, he raced to the rear for another cannonball, which he rolled into the muzzle. Marie Josephé repeated the ramming actions.

The gunner then used a long bar with a sharpened point to poke through the touchhole to expose the powder charge in the bore. Using a tube fashioned from a feather quill, he poured gunpowder to prime the charge, and shouted "*Amorce!*"

"*Prêt!*" Kirby was more than "*prêt*" to act this time. He and Marie Josephé stepped back from their positions in tandem and covered their ears.

"*Feu!*" The gunner touched the linstock with a slow match to the touchhole and lit the charge.

The haphazard team soon developed a rhythm to their movements, increasing in speed. The only conversation came from the gunner's shouted orders.

The sun dipped in the west. Fewer volleys passed between the two sides. The afternoon slipped into twilight as an eerie silence fell.

"*Vous avez été blessé.*" You have been hurt. Marie Josephé pointed to his right upper arm.

Kirby hunched his shoulder and peered at his coat. In addition to dirt and soot from the cannon, dark purple stains, almost black, covered his entire bicep area. Kirby shrugged from the coat and examined his shoulder. Much less blood covered the shirt. He ran his fingers under the collar and around his shoulder, finding no injury.

"*Ton bras saigne.*" Your arm is bleeding. The little boy ran to Kirby, eyes wide in alarm.

"I seem to be fine. I'm afraid it is blood on my sleeve from some of the soldiers." Apparently, his command of the French language only extended to comprehension. He could not utter a syllable in the language.

The gunner who had led their cannon crew came up to shake his hand.

"*Merci,*" he said, extending a hand.

"You're welcome," Kirby replied with a nod. He looked around the field. Prone bodies lay strewn in front of and at the sides of the cannons, while a few weary men sat propped with backs pressed against the wheels.

One by one, lanterns dotted the field. Streaks of smoke drifted across the air, still pungent with the odor of spent gunfire.

Kirby turned to Marie Josephé. "Can you get me a lantern? I'm a doctor. I can help the injured."

"Amable, *trouvez une lanterne, s'il vous plaît,*" Marie Josephé ordered. Find a lantern, please. "*Dis à ma sœur d'aider à évacuer les blessés.*" Tell my sister to bring help to move the wounded.

"*Oui, mademoiselle.*" The boy named Amable darted away.

Oddly, a lone church bell tolled, somewhere far in the distance, rolling over the hills. Heads turned in the direction of the unseen carillon. Kirby closed his eyes and braced for the anomaly that would transport him away. This episode had lasted the longest time between the bells.

When the fourth peal stopped reverberating, he opened his

eyes to find Amable at his side, holding a lantern. Kirby had changed neither time nor location.

CHAPTER 24

"No Time to Lose"

11th Toll of Midnight
Yorktown, Virginia 1781

Kirby took no time to reflect on what had just happened—or rather what had not happened. The gunner had returned to their group and spoke to Marie Josephé, his voice too low for Kirby to hear. She nodded but before she could relay the message, Amable lumbered into the circle, holding a lantern high, Louis just behind.

"Kirby, I am relieved to find you alive. I could not wake you when we arrived in the middle of the skirmish," his ancestor explained. "I shouted. Even the gunfire did not disturb you. I had to join in and found the wagon empty when I returned to it."

"It was the first time I slept since my—travels began," Kirby said. "But I did wake in time to see you run through the trees, and I followed. Two soldiers were killed. Mary Jo—I mean Marie Josephé took up the ramrod and I joined."

"Amable told us about the strange American who helped with the artillery. We are grateful for your assistance. "

"There are men out on the field. I must try to identify injuries," Kirby explained. "To see who is most seriously wounded, who is least, and those who we will not be able to save. Do you have a medical unit in your camp?"

"Not at our small camp, but we do have help coming. We will take the injured to the Americans. And I fear there will be many more wounded. Two assault parties have started an attack on this redoubt and another, the last two British defenses. They will fight with bayonets and hands, whatever is necessary to capture the redoubts. Once that is complete, we may conquer the enemy."

"You shall, my friend, you shall. Yorktown will fall, and Cornwallis will surrender. Now I must try to help with the wounded." Kirby grabbed the lantern and started moving from man to man, Marie Josephé and Amable at his heels. Louis and Francoise-Pierre fanned out to check their fallen comrades.

The group assessed the casualties. The first three men Kirby triaged had survivable shrapnel injuries; a fourth had burns received while trying to prime his artillery. Three more were dead. Two were alive but so severely wounded that they would not survive much longer. Marie Josephé remained with one, Francoise-Pierre with another to offer comfort until the men expired.

With Amable lighting the path, Kirby and Louis followed moans until they located one more man, dressed in civilian clothes, with a gunshot wound to the head.

"I need more light," Kirby called. Louis repeated the message in French and Amable brought the light closer. Hampered by the stingy shaft of light and lack of medical supplies, Kirby had limited ability to treat the injuries. He shrugged out of his wool coat and stripped free of his cotton shirt. He tore it into strips. Folding one strip into a compress and placing it on the wound, he told Louis to press gently. Kirby then wrapped a bandage across the man's head to hold it in place. The man groaned.

"This man has the most serious injury," Kirby said. "If we can get him to the hospital, maybe we can save him."

"Dinnae le' me die by the hands of those bloody bastards." The man's Scottish brogue thickened with the strain of speaking through his pain. He managed a weak smile that tightened into a grimace.

"*La civière!*" Louis called for a stretcher. He took the lantern and swung it in a wide arc. Two boys younger than Amable dragged a litter to their location.

Following Kirby's guidance, Louis and the three boys loaded the casualty onto the stretcher. Conversation mixed with groans as assistance reached the other wounded.

As the rescuers made their way through the thicket to waiting wagons, the sounds of battle picked up behind the redoubt. History would show that by morning, the American Army and their French allies would have the upper hand in the battle for Yorktown.

Throughout the early morning hours, Kirby worked in the primitive conditions of the army hospital. He first operated on the Scotsman, whose injury was less severe than first thought. Louis and Amable stayed close, assisting as best they could.

No one questioned Kirby's explanation that he had received medical training in the Navy. In a theater where supplies and personnel were lacking, any pair of hands was helpful. He offered advice for treatment, some of which the doctors followed, some not. The chaos increased as more and more wounded arrived from the hand-to-hand combat in the redoubts.

Amable disappeared at one point and returned with coffee for Louis and Kirby. The two older men took the cups.

"*Il faut que tu te reposes*, Amable," Louis said. You have to rest, Amable.

Kirby ruffled the boy's hair. Amable grinned, scooted to a corner of the tent, and sat out of the way. He drew his knees up and crossed his arms on top. Moments later, he cradled his head in his arms.

"Young Amable has watched you carefully through this night," Louis said as they sat side-by-side, backs against a tent pole. "He wants to become a doctor when he grows up. And I will tell you something else. When this war is over, I intend to become a doctor, and use my hands to heal lives, not end lives."

Kirby flashed a tired grin. "This may be the world's first case of an ancestor following in his descendant's footsteps."

"It would be amazing to live in your time, to see the things you have described. Do you have any idea how will you return to your world?"

"I don't know, Louis. I don't even know how I got here. I know the ring and the mirror must have had some connection to the midnight hour, and I had to be in the right place at the right time to get here to your world. I suppose I will have to be in the right place at the right time to get home. And I don't know where or when that is."

Louis sipped his coffee, then tilted his back against the pole. "I would not mind it if you stayed. Do you have anyone waiting at home for you? A wife, family?"

"Family, friends. No wife. I was engaged once but we called it off." Liana had barely crossed his mind since they broke up. Sandi's image popped into his head, and a slight smile crossed his features.

"But..." Louis prompted.

"Just before I—arrived here—I met someone. If I ever get back to her, I want to see where it will go. I think she will be the one. How about you, Louis? You got married, or I wouldn't be here."

"I love a girl. Her name is Lizzie."

Kirby nodded. "I know, Louis," he said. "And you will have a son named Phillip."

Shouts drowned the far-off sounds of fading battle. An American soldier burst through the tent flaps.

"We have captured the redoubts. Between the two assaults, almost two hundred British and Hessian soldiers were also captured."

A cheer followed. The cry—and the cheer—repeated as the soldier moved through the camp.

With victory all but assured, a jubilant group roused.

Although casualties continued to arrive at the hospital tent, the atmosphere was charged with anticipation and relief. Even some of the more seriously wounded were buoyed by the news. Sadly for some, death preceded the news.

With only short gaps of rest, Kirby spent another full day providing treatment as more wounded were brought in. Fresh medical teams arrived from other camps, and Kirby received the welcome news to go back to Louis' encampment.

Headed back to the French camp, unmindful of the wagon jerking and bouncing over ruts, Kirby smiled with the satisfaction of knowing what the immediate future would bring. As the battle-worn group pulled into the encampment, welcoming cheers rose, indicating news of the surrender had reached the camp. Drummers and fifers played lively tunes as children danced around. Soldiers clambered over the sides to meet welcoming arms of the adults. Women ran from the earthen ovens to greet the soldiers. The scents of baking bread and roasting meats drifted across the area, promising a celebratory feast.

Kirby was the last to disembark, remaining apart from the celebration. His body ached from hunching over the wounded, he was tired, hungry, and filthy. He had been in the same clothes for—how long? Since he had removed his shirt to make bandages, he had only worn the wool coat. Despite his frequent hand-washing, dried blood crusted at the wrists and splattered the front.

Louis walked to him. "You smell worse than a dog in a dung heap," he said.

"You're not much of a rosebud either, my friend. I'd kill for a shower right now."

Louis tilted back his head and roared with laughter. "Come with me. My father is not here but he will want to meet you when he gets in. We'll get you cleaned up." Louis motioned for Kirby to follow, leading him past rows of wedge-shaped tents to one of three larger shelters. He raised the flap. Amable stood in front of a wooden stand with a porcelain bowl, pouring a bucket of steaming water.

Nodding at Amable, Kirby said, "Oh, my God. Is that basin for me?" The next best thing to a shower!

"*Bon jour, monsieur*," the boy said. He raced over to Kirby and solemnly shook his hand, then grabbed the empty bucket and ran out of the tent.

"I am sorry we do not have better accommodations to offer you," Louis said.

"Are you kidding? This looks like a five-star hotel to me."

"I don't understand five-star."

"It means this is as perfectly fine as an elegant hotel. Thank you." Kirby eyed the single cot topped with a blanket and a fur skin. How long since he had slept in a bed?

Louis opened a trunk at the foot of the cot. He withdrew tan breeches similar to the grimy pair Kirby wore and handed them to him. He then found a button-less white shirt and tossed it over.

"You will find soap and a razor by the basin. Use the linen hanging there."

"Louis, I don't want to..."

"My father would expect nothing less than for me to offer you hospitality on his behalf." Louis bowed and stepped outside, folding the flap in pace.

Not wasting a second, Kirby shrugged free of the smelly wool jacket and plunged his hands into the clear, warm liquid. He scrubbed his arms and torso with a small bar of tan soap. Amable brought in another steaming pail. He set it down without a word and took the basin Kirby was using to empty. He returned and refilled the now empty vessel, steam rising once again. Before Kirby could say thanks, the boy dashed out, bucket clanging against the support pole.

Kirby rinsed and dried. He lathered his face as best he could and picked up the hand mirror.

He hardly recognized his own face. Brownish bruises lined the creases under his eyes, spreading to the still-swollen bridge of his nose. Dirt and grime streaked his skin, and his whiskers sported a lot more gray than he remembered. He lathered and began to shave, mindful of the scratches he'd received in his many escapades.

Amable reentered the tent with another bucket and repeated the movements he had made previously. He stood with the emptied pail and asked, *"Avez-vous fini, Monsier le docteur?"* Are you finished, Mr. Doctor?

"Oui, j'ai fini." Yes, I have finished. One of the few phrases he knew in French. He wiped the last of the soap from his jaw. *"Merci,* Amable."

The young boy stood, jaw gaping. "Louis!" He motioned around his own face. Kirby nodded and glanced in the looking glass. Other than the bruising, he could pass for an older version of Louis, or even a brother to Étienne. *I'm older than one great-grandfather, and nearly the same age as* his *father.*

"Il est l'heure de manger." It is time to eat. Amable backed away, gaze still transfixed on Kirby, and slipped outside without another word.

Kirby dressed in the clean shirt and breeches, feeling human again. He tidied the table and gathered his dirty clothes.

The aromas of baking and cooking set his mouth watering. Rows of tables were pushed together, laden with food. The gunner Francoise-Pierre rolled a barrel toward the table amid cheers from his colleagues. Sloshing indicated liquid contents.

A group of kids ran in circles. Three little girls broke free and circled Kirby with their hands clasped.

"Bonjour, Louis," a brown-haired child of about five cried as she danced in place.

"Bonjour, Louis," a second echoed. Kirby recognized Maggie, the same child he had seen at the clothesline. His jaw dropped as he watched Maggie and another little girl run toward the women, who were stoking fires at the earthen ovens.

"Hello, Kirby" the third little girl sang, and stopped before him, holding her arms out. "When did you get here?"

Kirby nearly fell over backwards as he stared into the earnest face of Sandi's daughter Norrie. Heart pounding in shock, he dropped to his knees and hugged her. "Norrie, how—when?" He looked over her shoulder. "Is your mother here?"

Norrie pointed toward the outdoor kitchen where the oldest sister, Theresé, ladled the contents of a black pot into a bowl Sandi held. When the bowl was filled, she carried it toward the table.

"Mommy!" Norrie shouted. Sandi set the dish down and looked in her daughter's direction. She went still when her eyes met Kirby's.

Kirby stood. His heartbeat roared in his ears, blocking every sound around him. His line of vision narrowed until everything was a blur except for the woman immobilized in front of him. Sandi took a step forward, stopped, then broke into a run.

Kirby met her halfway. She flew into his outstretched arms, skirts flowing as her twirled her around. Norrie clapped in excitement.

"My God, Kirby, is it really you?"

He set her on her feet but kept her in his embrace. Every ache disappeared, every tired bone strengthened, every part of his body came alive at her touch. *Every part.*

"How did you get here? When?" he asked.

"I don't know when. Weeks ago. Minutes ago. It began the night we came back from Busch Gardens. The clock struck midnight, with these jangling tolls that seemed to last forever. Norrie was gone from the bed. I found her in the living room, staring at the mirror. A strange greenish light glowed from the glass. Norrie was in a trance. I grabbed her, and we somehow got sucked into a tunnel of some sort. We landed in this camp, and the three sisters have been looking out for us. The older ones know where we came from, as if they expected us. They seem to have a special magic about them, something I can't explain. If Norrie hadn't been with me to make it real, I'd think I had gone crazy." She touched his cheeks. "Your poor face. What happened to you?"

Kirby shook his head. "It will take the whole night to tell you all that I have been through. But, Sandi, it is great to see you. I have to tell you something. I…"

A huge cheer erupted as horses clopped into the

177

encampment. Margaret and the first little girl ran to Norrie and grabbed her hand. The smallest of the three hugged a doll and said, "Come, Norrie, Papa has come back. We will celebrate now!" Giggling, the trio clutched their dolls as they chased each other in the direction of the new arrivals.

"The smallest girl. Is that Louis' youngest sister?"

Sandi nodded with a smile. "Nicole, Margaret, Norrie. Those three have become the proverbial three peas in a pod."

"I encountered Margaret in Portsmouth. Sandi, there is so much to tell you. Can we meet after this celebration?"

Louis called to Kirby to come with him.

"We'll find a way." Sandi trailed a finger along Kirby's jaw, and brought her hand to his shoulder. She moved in and brought her lips to his for a long, slow kiss before stepping back. She nodded once and walked over to where Marie Josephé and Theresé waited with several other women.

A French fifer played a tune that to Kirby sounded a lot like "For He's a Jolly Good Fellow." A drummer boy tapped along with a jovial rhythm. Soldiers from the camp lined up in formation to greet the arrivals. The smallest children gathered in a group on the opposite side.

Kirby joined several men in civilian clothes, who had formed a row in back of the Army formation. He immediately recognized Louis' father, who dismounted a white horse. Young Amable rushed to take the reins, a look of hero worship on his face. Other boys took the reins from two other high-ranking officers.

Étienne smiled, his face an older version of Kirby's own. Kirby wondered if the two officers accompanying his ancestor were Major General Baron De Viomenil, who history recorded as commanding the French attack on Redoubt 9, and the more famous Major General Marquis de Lafayette, who led the American charge on Redoubt 10.

Drum beats called the soldiers to attention and at ease several times in a row. Sometimes almost as soon the troops had come to attention, they were put at ease, then back to attention.

"I've never understood the French commands," the man beside Kirby muttered under his breath. "Attention and at ease, attention and at ease, over and over. Just bloody stand still." He angled his head toward Kirby and thrust a hand out. "I'm told ye are the one that saved my son. I'm Peter McDermott. My brother ferried you and Louis a few days ago. My boy was shot in the head at the redoubt, and they say 'twas ye that saved his life. I dinnae know how tae show my gratitude."

Kirby accepted the big Scots' hand clasp. "No need. Glad I was there to help."

The drummer tapped. The French soldiers snapped to attention. Another series of beats followed, and they stood at ease. Peter McDermott rolled his eyes.

The Marquis de Lafayette spoke. It took Kirby a second to understand the news, as the words were garbled by the cheering. Cornwallis had surrendered. The two major generals and their aides greeted each of the twenty-odd soldiers in the camp with a handshake and a few personal words. Young boys craned their necks to see while teenage girls swooned as the dashing young Marquis de Lafayette passed by.

Kirby's glance drifted from the parade area as he sought Sandi. She stood a few paces behind the other women, hands on Norrie's shoulders. The little girl danced on tiptoes and turned to say something to her mother. Sandi hesitated, then nodded. Norrie slipped to the front of the group and stood between Nicole and Margaret.

Sandi pulled the collar of a wool cloak around her neck and looked around until she caught Kirby's gaze. She smiled and turned back to the ceremony. Kirby continued his stare until she looked over her shoulder again. The shy smile turned to a coquettish grin, and his heart flipped, causing a stirring below his belly.

The drummer thumped the signal for attention.

Kirby was already at full attention and shifted his stance. He studied a loose thread on the jacket of the soldier in front of him, then the grass clump on the heel of his boot.

Anything to keep his mind off Sandi and the lewd and lascivious thoughts that had brought his body to attention.

***

After the two major generals shared a toast with the entire camp, they departed to the cheers and whistles of the small crowd. Fifers and drummers on foot accompanied the horsemen until they rounded a bend.

Louis found his way to where Kirby and Mr. McDermott stood. He carried a tray with three small pewter cups. He held it out to the others and each took one. Louis took the third, tucked the tray under one arm, and raised his hand in salute.

"Cornwallis sent a courier to deliver news of the British surrender. Generals Washington and Rochambeau are in Yorktown now finalizing terms. The surrender will take place in two days' time."

The three men raised their cups in toast and quaffed the whiskey. The warm liquor burned and soothed its way down Kirby's throat. McDermott clapped Louis on the shoulder. "Bloody good news indeed, laddie. But enough of this grape fer me. I've got a cask of *uisge-beatha* in me wagon. 'Tis time to break it open." The Scot thanked Kirby one more time and headed toward his wagon.

"Must be the barrel that nearly crushed me on the river crossing." Kirby chuckled.

Louis laughed and said, "My father would like you to come to his tent for a private meeting," When Kirby remained silent, he cleared his throat and continued. "He does not know that my mother died at Abigail's hands, nor Abigail at mine. He only knows that Mother succumbed to her illness. I've explained your appearances and what you told me as best as I could. Of course, he did not believe me at first. I told him about the victory, and how the blockade on the river prevented the British from getting supplies, which happened just as you said."

"Does he know who I am?"

"Yes. He will see for himself when you are face-to-face, as do I. The resemblance we three share is uncanny." Louis led the way to the commandant's tent, rapped once on a pole.

"*Entrez.*"

Louis lifted the flap and motioned for Kirby to come in.

Bare-chested to the waist, a towel slung over one shoulder, Commandant Étienne de la Rocher stood at the same wash basin Kirby had used earlier, pondering the results of his shave. He made eye contact with Kirby in the mirror and stopped short. He set the razor down, dried his chin, and reached for a clean shirt, buttoning it up before turning to face his descendant.

"My son says you come from many generations in the future. He has seen you many times throughout his life."

"I don't know how or why, but some occurrence caused me to leave my time and travel back to yours. I am a doctor, a Navy doctor, and we deal with science, not fantasy. Yet, here I am, your seventh great-grandson through Louis."

The commandant picked up a blue uniform jacket and brushed invisible lint from the wool. Kirby looked into the face he would wear in another five or so years. Laugh lines appeared at the corners of Étienne's eyes and mouth, but the burrows in his brow revealed the hardships he'd endured. Kirby realized that in real time, Clothiste's death had only occurred within the last few months. The man not only fought a war—he grieved for his wife and father.

"Can you go back to the time before my wife's death? Can you prevent it?"

Swallowing a lump in his throat, Kirby shook his head. "It doesn't happen under my control. I just end up wherever I am sent, at significant events in Louis' past life. I don't know if I will ever return to my own time, or how I will get back to it."

Étienne walked to him and extended his hand, his brilliant blue eyes never leaving his future great-grandson's. He stood an inch taller than Kirby's five feet ten. When Kirby reached to shake, Étienne hugged him instead.

"I'm told you saved the lives of many soldiers. You saved

the grandson of my father's best friend. I don't understand how this can even be possible, but I am happy to meet you, my—how many great-grandchildren are you?" He broke into a grin, a dimple appearing.

"There is a granddaughter in the twenty-first century, descended from Nicole. She has a dimple exactly like yours when she smiles."

The commandant withdrew a pocket watch and checked the time. "I must meet with my commanders in Yorktown soon. But I have time for you to tell me about my family in the twenty-first century. Louis, will you pour?" Louis nodded and retrieved a bottle of wine from a trunk.

Étienne shook his head. "For what we are about to hear, my son, I think it's best we open a bottle of McDermott's *uisge-beatha*. You will find it tucked amongst the wine bottles."

Outside, the celebrations grew noisier. Inside, father and son shared a bottle of whiskey with their progeny, who told them all about his family and the women who had descended from his daughters.

***

Kirby stretched his tired body on the commandant's cot. Before his sixth and seventh great-grandfathers—would he ever get used to that—had departed, Étienne had offered him his tent for the night.

Kirby had declined to join the celebration feast. He needed sleep more than he needed food or even water. He stripped from the borrowed breeches and shirt and slid under the blankets covering the cot.

The French encampment rang with excited voices. Every now and then a cheer arose. Then the soldiers would break into song. Some were accompanied by a lively fifer or drummer, others were more solemn, almost religious songs. Those melodies, low and slow, mesmerized Kirby and his eyes drifted shut.

A light tapping sounded at the tent pole. Kirby propped up

on his elbows and called, "Come in."

The flap parted, and Sandi pushed past the canvas, carrying a food-laden tray in one hand and holding a lantern in the other.

"I hope I didn't wake you," she said as she set both objects on the trunk.

"Not at all," Kirby lied. He sat up straight, bringing his knees to his chest and placing his arms on top.

"You must be exhausted. And starving." She sat on the edge of the trunk. Her concerned look took in the bruising along Kirby's ribcage, the black-and-blue marks from one elbow to the wrist.

"A little of both. That's some celebration out there."

Sandi nodded. "So much food out there. There's stew, some bread, and some kind of pastry Marie Josephé conjured up. Norrie wasn't happy she and the younger children had to go to bed. Isn't it amazing how much the sisters look like Mary Jo and Terry? And you are so much like Louis and his father, like a twin." She giggled. "I guess I could say a triplet. It makes you wonder if reincarnation isn't impossible."

Kirby nodded. "I'm almost ready to believe anything's possible now—even ghosts. But it is good to see you, Sandi. I've thought about you, wondering what if I never got back to the future? What if I never got to tell you how deeply I've fallen in love with you, how much I want to be with you?"

Sandi stood and walked the few paces to the side of the cot. Her eyes smoldered in the light as she pushed the covers aside. She lifted a knee and straddled Kirby's body, fluffing her skirt around her.

"Do you know what colonial women wear under their clothes?" she whispered. She leaned forward and brushed Kirby's cheek with a kiss, then whispered in his ear.

"Nothing—nothing at all."

Kirby decided as he wrapped his arms around Sandi, there are just some things a man needs more than sleep or food.

CHAPTER 25

"The Last Time"

12th Toll of Midnight
Portsmouth, Virginia Present Day

Following the trail of otherworldly sobs to the parlor, they entered the empty room. Stephanie stiffened. "It's here. Something happened in here." The crying repeated, seeming to come from every corner of the room. She ran toward the fireplace.

"Don't touch the candlesticks!" Terry shouted. The innocuous silver pair stood sentry on opposite sides of the fireplace mantle. She and Mary Jo had each experienced a series of unpleasant paranormal reactions when they first touched the silver candlesticks.

"They've never had any ill effect on me," Stephanie said. "One of you has to move them to see if you get a reaction."

"Our ghosts are gone, so I don't think anything will happen," Mary Jo said, striding up to the mantle. "But I'll try it." She flexed her fingers and grabbed both candlesticks at the same time.

Nothing happened. There were no vibrations, no burning metal against her skin.

Terry repeated Mary Jo's actions, with the same result.

Nothing happened.

"Okay, just to rule it out, I'll try too," Stephanie said. She performed the same movements the others had, with no result.

Low sobbing started, muffled and ethereal, the tearful sound fading in and out.

"Okay, that does it, I'm calling the police. It's nearly three a.m. and there's no sign of any of them in this house." Terry whisked her phone from her pocket.

"Look!" Stephanie pointed to the mantle clock. The minute hand began a slow rotation counterclockwise, the hour hand turning in the opposite direction. The movements sped up, and the arrows passed around the face of the clock in a wild spin, as if avoiding any possibility of coming together to meet the hour. The bric-a-brac on the mantle shimmied and danced in place as a low eerie glow washed over the mirror. The glass undulated.

The time indicators continued their duel and suddenly snapped to agreement at three o'clock. The women's reflections disappeared, and new shapes formed in their places. As if a faulty television screen had suddenly been turned on, three moving figures flickered inside the mirror's frame.

Kirby
Yorktown, October 19, 1781

Sandi's gentle breath brushed Kirby's skin as she nestled her head in the crook of his shoulder. He drew circles on her upper arm, wondering why it was such a sensual thing to do.

Between bouts of lovemaking, he had told her of his flashes in time, the somewhat painful journey from event to event. She had only to describe the relatively event-free travel she and Norrie had undergone, landing at dawn near the outdoor ovens where Marie Josephé and Theresé prepared food for the day.

"I didn't have to explain much," Sandi said. "The girls, especially Theresé, seemed to be expecting someone, perhaps Terry or Mary Jo. They gave us clothes, and we were just accepted in the camp. We learned to cook in the outdoor ovens and had to wash clothes by hand. I've enjoyed this experience, Kirby, even though it won't be something I can talk about when I get home. Except to the Dunbar family, of course."

"I guess that includes me, then, since I am some kind of distant cousin to them all?"

"Of course," Sandi laughed.

"Explain one thing to me, though. What were you wearing when you arrived here?"

"Yoga pants and a t-shirt. Why"

"What happened to your underwear?"

Sandi rolled on top of him. In a whiskey voice, she said, "I must have been practicing to be a colonial woman. And we have a few minutes more before everyone figures out where I am."

"They probably know where you are," Kirby said as he settled Sandi in a most comfortable position. "Let's give them something to talk about."

***

Throngs of people lined both sides of the streets as Kirby escorted the daughters of Commandant Étienne de la Rocher to a small clearing where rows of French soldiers stood at attention. During the walk to the parade area, Kirby had taken notice of the stone-faced British soldiers waiting in haphazard clusters in and around the town center. Interspersed with small pockets of German troops, the men wore dejected expressions, or glared at the burgeoning crowds. A few drank from flasks they passed back and forth. Drummers thumped listless music befitting a funeral dirge.

Norrie, Margaret, and Nicole played a game of tag, skipping in and out of the civilian crowds. Each time one of the youngsters tagged another, they stopped to exchange dolls.

Sandi corralled the girls and had them walk beside her.

Family members of a number of French officers were already in the clearing and greeted the new arrivals with nods and smiles. Kirby bowed as he delivered Theresé and Marie Josephé to their designated area.

"Are you sure you will not stand with us as we witness the

surrender of the British army?" Marie Josephé asked.

Kirby shook his head. "Nothing would make me prouder than to stand with my French family, but we think it is more appropriate for us to join the ranks of the Americans for this event."

"We understand. It will not be long now before the celebrations begin." Theresé smiled, although tears glistened in her eyes.

"May I stay with the Americans?" Margaret asked.

"Of course." Theresé nodded. The two older sisters each held out a hand toward Nicole and called her to them.

Nicole hugged the other two little girls tightly. "Good bye, Norrie, goodbye Margaret," she said with a giggle.

"Goodbye, Nicole," Norrie and Margaret answered in unison, holding hands as they clutched their dolls in their free arms.

Nicole next hugged Sandi, then held her arms up to Kirby. He lifted her in his arms and she buried her head in his shoulder, whimpering softly.

"We will see you this afternoon after the ceremony, little one," he said, patting her arm.

Nicole shook her head emphatically. "No. I won't have the chance to say goodbye later. I love you, Kirby."

"I love you too, Nicole." *My sweet little sixth great-grand aunt.*

Theresé and Mary Josephé looked at each other and nodded. Therese spoke as a shudder rippled through her. She tightened her cloak around her throat. "Nicole is right. I feel—something. Let us say goodbye as well, in case we shall not see you again." She hugged the little girls, then Sandi. When she embraced Kirby she whispered, "Thank you for all you have done for our family, especially for Papa and Louis." She stepped back and joined hands with her sisters.

After goodbyes were exchanged, Kirby guided his small entourage to the American side. He led them toward a grassy knoll that allowed a vantage point of the historic ceremonies that would soon take place in front of them.

A few minutes before twelve, Kirby entwined his fingers

with Sandi's and pulled her close. "I've been waiting for the twelfth toll. Don't let go of my hand," he cautioned. She nodded and tightened her grip on Norrie's arm.

They waited with the crowd, the air heavy with anticipation.

Far away, a church bell tolled the first note in the noon hour. Nearby, a young boy held up a triangle musical instrument. He shouted, "Twelve o'clock and all's well," using a metal wand to strike the sides of the copper frame. He matched time with the church bell, the echoing vibrations wafting over the air. As the collective clangs announced the hour, Kirby steeled himself in preparation for yet another journey back in time.

None of the painful pulling or twisting occurred that precipitated his usual entry into the time vortex. When the church bell and the triangle silenced, murmurings of anticipation rippled through the growing hordes.

Kirby relaxed—yet his heart sank. *Have I reached the end of the journey, and I'm now stuck in this time forever?* He glanced sideways at Sandi's profile, down her neck and to the swell of her breasts above her gown. A jolt of pure desire shot to his loins, clouding his mind from everything except one thought. *I can face anything with this woman at my side.*

"It didn't work." Sandi turned and caught his gaze as his eyes traveled the upward journey to her face. She arched an eyebrow. "See something you like, Doctor?"

"I do indeed, Madame." He released her fingers and angled his elbow toward her.

Muffling a giggle at his formal tone, Sandi slid her hand in the crook of his arm. "You sound like a colonist now."

"I think I've become one. How long have I been back in time now? It seems like forever. But that's the second time that tolling bells did not send me to another flashback. Now I am worried that we may be stuck in this time zone for all eternity."

"Oh, please don't tell me that. I'm craving a good long shower and soft soap. That lye soap is killing my skin."

Kirby's eyes crinkled as he stifled a laugh. He sobered and frowned. "Damn. I thought we'd finally be heading home when that church bell tolled. I don't know what to expect now," he whispered. "Only time will tell—pun intended."

"Then I guess we better turn our attention to the history unfolding before us." Sandi inched closer to Kirby as more people joined the pressing throngs.

Far down one side of the street, out of view, a lone male voice shouted "Forward, march," over the din of the crowd. Fifes shrilled, and drumbeats pounded a steady tattoo. Thousands of marching feet beat a steady cadence that grew louder with each step. The crackle of leaves crunching underfoot added a new cadence to the marching tunes.

When the first soldiers on horseback appeared, the crowds roared with approval. The combined American and French armies marched past the crowds and soon formed single files on opposite sides of the road. Each regiment in turn completed a left or right face maneuver accordingly so that they faced each other.

The French were decked out in full uniform. White woolen uniform pants and belts, blue or white jackets with a multitude of insignia, gold braids and brass buttons identified ranks and regiments. Buffed medals reflected in the sunlight.

In contrast, many of the American soldiers were attired in a mishmash of clothes—uniforms, partial uniforms, and civilian dress. However, what they wore was clean and polished. The men stood in formation, erect and proud. Bands from both armies took turns playing lively music. Officer's plumes waved in the breeze, dancing in time with the crisp flap of regimental flags proudly carried by standard bearers. Soldiers on both sides wore freshly brushed tricorn hats, many adorned with knots of ribbons.

"What are those knotted things on the men's hats, Mommy?" Norrie asked.

"I don't know, honey," Sandi answered.

"They're called cockades," Kirby explained.

Sandi glanced at him, lifting an inquisitive eyebrow.

Kirby shrugged. "I did a thesis about the Revolutionary War. You pick up a lot of sidebars of information when you research."

"Mommy, the soldiers are lined up as far as I can see." Norrie stood on tiptoes as she peered down the road.

"I can't see," Margaret complained from her position between Kirby and Sandi. She held both her doll and Norrie's, twisting her wrists to engage the dolls in a puppet-like dance.

Kirby knelt with his back to Margaret, and she scrambled on his shoulders. Both dolls smacked his head as she steadied herself.

"Hey, watch it with the dolls, girlie," Kirby admonished. Margaret giggled as she settled her legs, her petticoat covering Kirby's eyes. She handed one of the dolls to Norrie.

"Now I can't see." Kirby held one hand in front of him, the other anchoring Margaret's knee.

Sandi laughed as she settled Margaret's underskirt behind Kirby's neck. "And look, girls, you can see General Washington on his magnificent horse."

The crowds' murmurs rose to a crescendo. Necks craned as all eyes in the crowd sought the impressive figure of General Washington guiding his noble courser to the head of the American line. Several of his aides surrounded him. Count Rochambeau rode into place beside Washington, but at the head of the French army. Both men shook hands. The crowds roared with approval.

Civilians jostled closer, filling every available space behind either army.

Led by officers on horseback, the British Army began their dejected advance through the columns of enemy soldiers. Although dressed smartly, the soldiers shuffled leaves underfoot as they moved listlessly. With colors furled and encased, in sharp contrast to the multitude of triumphant flags snapping along the path, the men marched out-of-step, weapons shouldered, and often broke ranks in drunken weaves.

The lead British officer rode toward the two victorious generals. Ignoring Washington, he faced Rochambeau and doffed his hat.

"Lord Cornwallis sends the message that he is unwell and regrets he will not attend the surrender ceremony. I am his second in command, General Charles O'Hara." He offered his sword in surrender.

The Comte de Rochambeau set a rigid jaw and directed General O'Hara to General Washington.

O'Hara turned to the American commander. Stalwart and firm, General Washington stared the surrendering general down. "General Lincoln shall accept the surrender." His named subordinate moved forward and took the sword from the British officer in the ceremonial move, then returned it.

O'Hara turned to his men and said, "Ground arms." Any semblance of dignity dissipated as the soldiers responded to the order by tossing their weapons into a pile. Several attempted to bash the arms to render them useless, but stopped on command of General Lincoln.

Kirby whispered to Sandi, "Cornwallis could not show his face to the surrender, and 'called in sick.' He sent a secondary officer. It was a rather pointed insult that the general tried to admit defeat to the head of the French troops rather than the American commander. Rochambeau did the right thing in directing him to Washington, but ultimately it was Washington who had the last laugh by directing the surrendering general to his own subordinate."

The parade of soldiers surrendering their arms continued for several minutes. Kirby recognized the surly face of the guard who had threatened him in the Portsmouth prison. As the scruffy man tossed his rifle into the pile, he glanced around and made eye contact with Kirby.

Kirby drew his forefinger across his throat and the guard lowered his gaze before shuffling behind his colleagues.

"That soldier was guarding prisoners in Portsmouth." Kirby jutted his chin in the man's direction. "Too bad that he is being allowed to return to England instead of being taken prisoner of war. What a hellhole that jail was. I hope that Louis will see to it that those imprisoned men are cared for."

"We are truly witnessing history in the making." Sandi

remarked

"That's what my daddy said when he took us to see the president," Margaret said, peering at Kirby.

Kirby tilted his head to look up at the little girl and gently tugged a curl on her forehead. "How could you see him when he hasn't been…how did you see President Washington?"

Margaret tipped her head over Kirby's. With a hand on either side of his face, she tilted his face toward hers. Crossing her upside-down eyes as she looked into his, she laughed again and said, "Not him, silly. President Lincoln." She straightened and clapped her hands to the tempo of the music.

Kirby and Sandi glanced at each other, exchanging inquiring looks.

The young boy with the triangle musical instrument moved closer. He struck the sides, shouting as the first clang rang out, "Three o'clock and all's well." He ran several feet further and poised to repeat the actions in front of Kirby.

Clang.

The ground trembled beneath Kirby's feet. Locking one arm over Margaret's knees, he linked arms with Sandi. She in turn reached for Norrie, circling her arm around her daughter's waist.

"Hold on," he shouted.

Clang.

Gale-force winds sucked them into the vortex, spinning them like bullets shooting from a gun. The little girls screamed. The violent winds lifted Margaret off of his shoulders and he managed to catch her ankle before she sailed away. His and Sandi's bodies smacked into each other several times before their hands broke apart and he lost his grip on Margaret.

They spiraled down a long dark tunnel, their path only lighted by the sporadic opening of doors that immediately slammed shut.

One light burned at the end of the tunnel, dimming and lighting as shadows passed behind it. He and Sandi bumped again as they propelled toward the light. Norrie drifted by, giggling as she passed away from his outstretched hand.

"Kirby!" Muffled voices called his name, the shouts growing louder the nearer he got to the portal. The opening undulated like a roaring waterfall. Human forms developed behind the opaque partition.

Hands plunged through the rippling square. Kirby reached for one, Sandi the other. Superhuman strength pulled them to the fore. Kirby bumped into Sandi one more time as they shot through the square light and crash-landed in the 21st century.

The collective arms of Terry, Mary Jo and Stephanie pulled with all the force they could muster, falling backwards as their targets popped from the mirror. Humans rolled into a pile, knocking aside furniture and sending the table lamp crashing to the floor.

Kirby scrambled to his feet first, helping Terry, upon whom he had landed, to hers. Mary Jo was sprawled with her back against the wing chair, Stephanie leaning into her shoulder. She stood on unsteady legs, extending her hand to Mary Jo to help her up.

Sandi rolled on her back with her child still gripped tightly in her arms.

"Mommy!" Norrie's voice warbled.

"Norrie!" Sandi screamed. All eyes turned to her panicked face staring at the child she held.

The little girl in the flowered pinafore was not Norrie.

Margaret had traveled with them into the future.

"MOMMY!" The shout emanated from the quivering mirror over the fireplace. Green light flickered over the group of people before the mirror hardened back to glass and reflected their stunned faces.

Norrie was now the child who was lost in time.

CHAPTER 26

"Child in Time"

Portsmouth, Virginia Present Day

"My baby! Where's my baby girl?" Sandi screamed. She set Margaret to one side and scrambled to her feet, racing to stand in front of the fireplace.

"Norrie, are you in there?" She slapped her hands against the solid surface of the mirror, her anguished face staring at the reflections of others in the room. Her knuckles turned white as she gripped the mantle.

Kirby joined Sandi in front of the fireplace. He tapped fingertips all over the glass, to no avail.

"I'm right here, Mommy." Norrie's voice warbled, muffled in the distance and edged with a tinny tone. "Where are you?"

"I'm here, baby girl, trying to find you. Don't be afraid."

"I'm not, Mommy. I'm going to play with the other kids." The distant peals of children's laughter echoed as Norrie's words faded.

"No, Norrie, stay right there. Don't go away." Sandi's voice cracked. Kirby slipped his arm across her shoulder. She turned her face inward and stifled a sob against his chest. A cacophony of voices shouted questions as Terry, Mary Jo, and

Stephanie joined them.

"What happened?"

"Where have you been?"

"Why are you dressed like that?"

"Are you okay?"

"Who is this little girl?"

Former Army sergeant Mary Jo put her fingers to her teeth and took control with a shrill whistle. Silenced, the others turned their heads in her direction.

"One at time, guys. First thing—is everybody all right? Physically, I mean." She touched Sandi's shoulder but looked at Margaret. The little girl sat on the floor, eyes wide as she clutched her doll to her chest.

Sandi, still in Kirby's embrace, swallowed hard and nodded. She moved aside, gaze locked on the mirror. Kirby walked toward Margaret and knelt beside her.

"Are you okay, Margaret?" he asked, tone gentle.

Margaret nodded and looked around the room. "Where am I now? Is this Auntie Celestine's house?"

"Margaret, do you know where Norrie is?"

"No. Is she lost-ed like I am?"

Kirby nodded. "I think she may be. Have you been lost for a long time, Margaret?"

She lifted one shoulder in a shrug, hugging the doll closer. Kirby rose and walked back to Sandi. He rubbed his hand along her arm.

The clock struck once on the quarter hour after three o'clock.

"What day is this?" he asked.

"It's Sunday." Terry said. "We've been here for the last twelve hours. After we got here and found the house empty, the clock went crazy at three a.m. We could see something in the mirror, and then it faded away. We decided that we should wait until three this afternoon to see if that was a clue to a significant time."

"But it's still the Sunday after Thanksgiving, right, Terry?" When she bobbed her head in affirmation, he continued.

"Fifteen hours' time has passed since this all started at midnight Saturday. I can't explain it yet, but somehow, we—me, Sandi, Norrie—got caught in a time warp. And Margaret too. Sandi and I made it back to our time, but Norrie did not. And neither did Margaret make it back to her time."

"Okay, this is too much." Mary Jo held her hands, palms out. "We know everyone is okay, but we need to figure out what is going on. We're going to sit down and start at the beginning." She turned her head. "Stephanie, can you put on a pot of strong coffee for us, please?"

"I'm on it," Stephanie said and went toward the kitchen.

"I'll help you." Terry followed.

"Come sit down, Sandi," Mary Jo said, trying to draw her friend away from the fireplace.

Sandi shook her head. "I'll stay here near the mirror, in case…" Tears rolled down her face. "In case Norrie…"

"It's going to be okay," Kirby said. "We'll get her back, Sandi. We got back here. I'll be with you through all of this and together we'll find a way."

"But she's just a baby, Kirby. Will she even know how to get back if she can? I've never not known where she was. Ever since she was born, I've known exactly where she was, every minute."

"We'll figure it out, Sandi." Kirby circled his arms around Sandi and drew her closer.

Mary Jo caught the subtle movement of Sandi touching her forehead to Kirby's before dropping her hand to his shoulder. Keeping her eyes averted, Mary Jo straightened the tables that had been displaced, gathering the family papers that had been scattered when the time travelers blew back into the present.

Terry walked back into the room, carrying a tray laden with mugs, creamer and sugar bowl. On her heels, Stephanie brought in the coffee pot and another mug,

Upon catching the eyes of her friends, Mary Jo inclined her head toward the embracing couple. Stephanie raised a curious eyebrow, but turned her attention to Margaret and said, "Margaret, would you like some hot chocolate?"

"Thank you, ma'am," the little girl replied. She set the doll to the side and held her hands out for the cup.

"Okay, let's begin at the beginning," Mary Jo ordered. She sat on the couch between Stephanie and Terry, opposite Sandi and Kirby in matching wing chairs.

Stephanie sat poised to write, pen and pad in hand. When Mary Jo arched an eyebrow, Stephanie said, "Hey, you know I keep track of everything with my lists. Kirby, what was the first event that happened?"

"Well, Friday night, I arrived at the inn and had no issues," Kirby said. "The lady who checked me in showed me around and then she went back to her own room. I went out for dinner with friends and returned just as the clock struck midnight. I thought I saw strange lights in the parlor, reflecting in the mirror." All eyes turned in the direction as Kirby glanced to the big frame.

"Kirby made so much noise that I thought it was someone breaking in," Sandi interrupted. "I'm afraid me and my forty-five greeted him. But even though we sat talking for hours, waiting each time the clock struck on the hour, nothing else happened so we went to our rooms. We got up early and spent the next day at Busch Gardens, and got home kind of late. I got Norrie to bed and settled. Then I thought I heard a child crying. But Norrie was fine."

"Crying woke me up too," Kirby said. "I thought it was Norrie and came downstairs to check, but everything was quiet. Then the clock hit midnight and all hell broke loose. The candlesticks rattled, the hands of the clock twirled. Next thing I knew, I got sucked into the time warp."

Sandi added, "I had gotten up to go to the bathroom and all was fine. I heard Norrie call—at least I thought she'd called—but when I came into the bedroom she wasn't in her bed. The midnight chimes were still tolling, but it seemed as if the sounds were in slow motion. Each stroke of midnight clanged incessantly, lasting longer and longer. I ran out of the bedroom and found Norrie walking toward the fireplace. I snatched her in my arms right at the toll of the fifth bell, and then we were whisked into the mirror."

Three pairs of eyes stared wide. Terry paused with her coffee mug half-way to her lips.

"It took me a little while to realize what was happening to me," Kirby said. "Each time the clock struck the hour, I was transported to a different scene in Louis' life. I saw the day he was born, as well as other events in his youth. Even though *they* were the ghosts and I could see them, no one could see me, except the little kids. However, Louis always seemed to sense my presence at each event. We would somehow make eye contact and then I was poofed to the next event." Kirby relayed each of the events he had witnessed, trying to keep his memories in as chronological an order as possible. He detailed the experiences from the first episode, up until the moment he had climbed the steps to reach the injured Abigail.

The others remained silent as he took a gulp of coffee. He rotated the mug in his hands. "I saw what happened here in this house the night Abigail and Clothiste died. Louis didn't kill Abigail, Terry. He had every intention of killing her when he choked her, but she was still alive when I reached her. Even though he had killed in the line of duty, her death had haunted him all of these years, apparently trapping him in between life and death."

Terry and Mary Jo both started to ask questions and Stephanie interrupted. "Wait, I'm almost caught up." She scribbled furiously. "I have a million questions, as I'm sure we all do."

"Let's save the questions until they've finished," Terry suggested.

Kirby continued. "A new time travel sucked me away from the scene with Louis and Abigail, but when I came back, time had only advanced to the next night. Louis had already buried Abigail in the early morning hours and hidden in the outside kitchen. Theresé arrived on a search for her mother. He and Theresé then devised a plan to make it look like Louis had been attacked in order to account for his disappearance from his unit. I dropped in from nowhere-land just about the time she was wielding a board to knock him out. I dropped in just at that moment. She clipped me with the board and Louis, now seeing me in person, belted me with two good punches." Kirby described the scenes at the jail and the escape across the James River.

Sandi took up the story. "Norrie and I didn't go through all of the time changes that Kirby experienced. We landed at the camp with the three sisters. Even without me showing up in yoga pants and t-shirt, Therese knew right away we were not from her world. She helped us, found clothes for us, protected us. Finally, Kirby arrived, although with his black eyes and swollen face I didn't recognize him right away. He helped save the lives of many men."

"It is a wonder anyone survived the practices of the eighteenth century. Louis watched me work and decided to become a doctor when the war was over. I was finally able to tell him that Abigail had not died as he thought, and he got some comfort from that. Then we received the news that Cornwallis would surrender. We even saw Washington and the French leader Rochambeau ride on their horses, and we witnessed the British lay down their weapons and capitulate."

"Kirby had Margaret on his shoulders, and he said we were watching history in the making. That's when Margaret said her daddy said the same thing when he took her to see the president. That really confused us, because Washington was not even president yet. When Kirby asked what she thought of President Washington, she laughed and said she was talking about President Lincoln. Then we got zapped back here."

Everyone turned to look at Margaret, who had fallen asleep with the mug of chocolate still in her hand. Stephanie stepped over and removed the mug, scooped the little girl up and laid her on the couch. She reached to pick up the doll and Sandi cried out.

"She has Norrie's doll." Sandi clamped her hand to her mouth, then glanced at Kirby. "They were switching their dolls back and forth while we watched the parade."

Kirby scratched his jaw, fingers raking across his five

o'clock shadow. "They must have been holding each other's dolls when that kid announced three o'clock and clanged that metal triangle. Maybe that is what caused them to change places, because Norrie's doll Maggie belonged in the twenty-first century. That other doll belonged in—whatever time Margaret came from."

"She mentioned Abraham Lincoln?" Stephanie asked. "And her name is Margaret?"

Kirby and Sandi nodded in unison.

Stephanie shuffled through papers on the coffee table. Brow furrowed in concentration, she grabbed her phone and swiped the screen while she talked. "Maggie is the name of the little girl who disappeared here in eighteen sixty-one. You all do know that Maggie is short for *Margaret*, right?" She waited until everyone in the room looked her way and nodded in agreement. She added, "Kirby, if I am right—meet your great-great-grand aunt Margaret Lawrence."

"What makes you think that, Stephanie?" Kirby asked.

"Lincoln was sworn into office on March four, eighteen sixty-one. The letter describing Maggie's disappearance was dated April, eighteen sixty-one. No specific date."

"Oh, my God, this gets worse and worse." Sandi pressed her fingers to her temples.

"No, wait, don't give up yet," Stephanie cautioned. "You may think I am crazy, but this was meant to happen, just like when the girls' ghosts appeared to us. We found the jewels and helped them solve mysteries, right?"

"I see where you're going with this, Steph," Terry said. "We're somehow the key to getting Margaret back to her time, which will bring Norrie home to her time. And we have Kirby now, who is the link to Margaret and her family."

"But if the mirror is the portal and it's closed, how will we get them back?" Sandi asked. She did not look up, merely remained in place with her hands still to her temples.

Stephanie shook her head. "I don't know yet, Sandi. There might be a clue in the letters."

"Three o'clock," Kirby said. He raised his index finger and

shook it, his brow furrowed with thought.

"What do you mean, three o'clock?" Sandi dropped her hands and stared at Kirby.

"All of my events happened in connection with the clock striking twelve. Several were when the clock chimed at midnight, but several others occurred at noon. Except for the last episode. Remember, at the surrender, Sandi? Noon passed, and we braced for action, but nothing happened. Later, the young boy was announcing 'three o'clock and all is well' and he clanged on that triangle instrument. That's when we came home."

"That's right. So, you think maybe something will happen at the next three o'clock that will bring Norrie back, Kirby?" The hope in Sandi's voice tugged at Kirby's heart.

"I don't know, Sandi. It's just a thought. There has to be some kind of key to opening the time warp, something we have to identify so we can be ready."

"Sandi, I still have many more letters and journals to go through that might offer a clue," Stephanie said. "I will search everything referencing that time frame. But I want to mention something. In the letter that talked about Margaret disappearing, Celestine said that it had been two days without a sign of the missing child. Whatever caused her to disappear, we know that she had been missing for at least two days. And…oh my God. I just remembered something." Stephanie paced back and forth, rubbing her temples as she concentrated.

"What is it, Stephanie?" Kirby asked.

In response, Stephanie swiveled on her heel and faced Terry and Mary Jo. "It happened shortly after I moved here. We were preparing for Hurricane Abigail, and it was early afternoon. Gage and I were taking supplies to the apartment. Something by the magnolia caught my attention. Some of the leaves turned inward, and there was a light wind rustling branches at the bottom. It was so strange to see the top portion motionless. Not a single top branch moved, just the lower limbs. I remember thinking they waved like a person beckoning for help."

"Not to be short with you, Stephanie, but what has that got to do with anything right now?" Mary Jo asked.

"I'm getting to it, Mary Jo," the usually tranquil Stephanie snapped. "I remember seeing a small girl's shape by the tree, but she vanished. Then, once Nicole started appearing to me in the apartment, I just assumed her first appearance was at the tree. But now..." Stephanie glanced at the sleeping Margaret. "Now I think it might really have been Margaret I was seeing."

"So, the hour of three o'clock and a storm might be what it takes to get Norrie back to our time?" Mary Jo asked, her tone a little softer.

"I don't know. It seems logical." Stephanie shook her head. "Maybe we can find out what happened when Margaret wakes, without scaring her to pieces."

"Terry, I'm not coming to work tomorrow." Sandi walked to the fireplace and ran her fingers along the mirror glass again. "I have to stay tonight, see if anything happens at three in the morning. I can't leave my baby here, alone."

Terry crossed the room and clasped Sandi's shoulder. "Hey, don't worry about the office. We can handle anything there. Take as much time as you need here at the inn. If need be, we'll cancel the reservations for the upcoming weekend."

"Let's see what happens during the night. I'll be here, in case..." Sandi swallowed and shook her head once before looking at Stephanie. "Steph, can I look through those papers, see if I can find something in them?"

"Of course. And we need to get the guys here. We don't know what might happen, and I can't keep this from Gage any longer." Stephanie stood and walked over to her files. She handed them to Sandi.

Terry nodded. "I agree, they should know. But I don't think we should tell anyone else right now. What do you say we all meet back here at six o'clock? We'll bring food and discuss what we need to do." She stopped short and pointed to Sandi's dress.

"Look at your clothes. They're disintegrating."

Sandi glanced at her skirts. The cottony material darkened

and crinkled with age, turning almost translucent.

"And the bruises on your face, Kirby," Mary Jo added. "They've almost faded away."

"Everything is in our own time now," Kirby said. His breeches were holding up rather well, but the loose cotton shirt and waist-coat he wore started to dilapidate. "These clothes are almost two hundred and forty years old and would probably not have survived, so they will be disappearing. I best get up to my room and to my twenty-first century duds before I'm standing before you in the altogether."

"Nothing to see here," Mary Jo quipped. She shaded her eyes, peeking through her fingers as Kirby scooted past and hit the stairs running.

Sandi hugged her law partner. "Thank you, Terry. All of you."

Terry returned the hug, then ran her palms down Sandi's arms until their hands clasped. "Listen, try not to worry. As unbelievable as it is, you and Kirby, and Margaret..." she glanced at the sleeping youngster, then back. "All of you have traveled in time and come back safely. Okay, I know Margaret is still displaced, but we just have to find the key to switch her and Norrie."

A giggle escaped from the wall. Sandi looked at the fireplace. The clock's hands clicked around the face in normal tempo. The mirror reflected normal images. The giggle continued until it faded to silence.

She sighed, fighting back tears. "I have to believe that, Terry. I have to."

"Well, you're nearly naked. Go take a shower. Try to relax. We'll be back with the troops and figure this out. And maybe you can loan Margaret something of Norrie's to replace her dress."

Sandi nodded. "I have something in my room." As her friends walked with her toward the innkeeper's suite, she glanced one more time over her shoulder.

Afternoon sunlight filtered through the window slats, shining on a silent, still room.

EPILOGUE

Sandi grabbed clean clothes and dashed into the shower. She wanted to be close to the parlor in case there were any signs from Norrie. But the hot water and glorious glycerin soap brought much needed relief as she scrubbed her skin. She lathered shampoo, skipping conditioner. As the suds rolled down her shoulders, she pressed her palms against the tile wall.

"Please, God, let my baby be safe. Send her home to me," she prayed.

A peaceful feeling seemed to wash over her with the flowing water. Whatever needed to be done, she had good friends to help her. She glanced toward the ceiling above, where Kirby's bedroom and bath were.

And with him at her side, she would make it through this.

***

Kirby showered, closing his eyes and wishing that Sandi could be with him as the hot water rained down on him. His heart thumped its now familiar tap dance in his chest. He prayed that Norrie and Margaret could return to their right places in time, so that he could pursue a future with the lawyer and her daughter.

He stepped from the shower and wrapped a towel around his waist. He peered in the mirror. The image staring back looked nearly normal, other than some slight yellowing under his eyes and on his torso. The fatigue had eased, the aches had disappeared.

He walked to the bedroom and sat on the bed, his gaze falling to the table where his wallet, cell phone and other pocket paraphernalia scattered around the lamp. He buckled the watchband around his wrist and checked the time. Four-thirty.

He ignored the wallet and pile of change, having no use for either at the moment. He picked up his cell phone, smiling as he remembered trying to explain the device to Louis.

"What would you think of my world, Grandfather Louis?" he asked aloud. He saw the indication that he had missed incoming calls, many with numbers he didn't recognize as he scrolled through the list. He punched his voicemail code.

Stephanie's shaky voice was the first message. "Kirby, I'm sorry to bother you. We can't get hold of Sandi, and now you. Have you made it back from Busch Gardens safely? We're just awfully worried. Could you call me as soon as you get this message? It doesn't matter what time. Please call."

Similar messages followed from Terry and Mary Jo. One call from his colleague Dr. Murphy O'Shea informed him that Seaman Trevor Wilson was moved to the orthopedic ward. Kirby made a mental note to return Murphy's call as soon as he finished checking his missed calls.

His mom left word they would be home December third and wanted to visit him a week later. There were a couple of messages from the civilian doctors with whom he had interviewed, asking him to call on Monday.

Finally, he reached the last message. The screen showed he had missed four calls from the same number, but there was only one voicemail.

"Kirby, this is Liana. You need to call me." She paused. Kirby rolled his eyes and pressed the bridge of his nose with his thumb and forefinger as he waited.

"Call me. I'm pregnant."

The phone clicked, and voicemail told him there were no more message in his mailbox.

KIRBY'S FAMILY TREE

Elisabeth (unk 1st wife) m. PHILLIPE DE LA ROCHER (aka Phillip Rocker) m. Abigail Weldon (2nd wife)
/

ÉTIENNE DE LA ROCHER (1743-1812 age 69) m. CLOTHISTE JANVIER (1748[1]-1781 age 33)
/

LOUIS ÉTIENNE ROCHER dit LAWRENCE (1763-1860) m. Elizabeth "Lizzie" Wheeler
/

PHILLIP LAWRENCE (1785-1841) Sadie O'Connell, second wife Penny Gagnon[2]
/

LEWIS LAWRENCE (1807-1833) m. Mary Jane Dodd[3]
/

DANIEL PATRICK LAWRENCE (1833-1927) m. Martha "Lauralee" Stalls[4]
/

FRANK MICHAEL LAWRENCE (1854-1899) m. Kathleen Pulley
/

JACK LAWRENCE (1900-1979) m. Antoinetta Guilette
/

ANTHONY LAWRENCE (1927-2000) m. Elizabeth Gould
/

PATRICK LAWRENCE (1954-) m. Rachel Benning
/

KIRBY DANIEL LAWRENCE (1980 -) engaged to Sandi K. Cross (1984-)

---

[1] Kyle and Stephanie's research uncovered several incorrect birthdates in Stephanie's original records. Clothiste was actually born in 1748. Louis was born in 1763, Theresé in 1764, and Marie Josephé in 1765.

[2] Phillip went to Ireland, had son Lewis with Sadie, widowed, had twins Étienne and Clothiste with Penny

[3] Lewis was born in Ireland, (after his death, wife Mary Jane brought Daniel to America at age 4)

[4] twin boys Frank Michael and Jack Wayne Lawrence, daughter Margaret

TURN THE PAGE
FOR A SNEAK PREVIEW OF

CHILD OF TIME
The Pearl Story

PROLOGUE

Portsmouth, Virginia 1861

My name is Margaret and I am eight. I shouldn't have taken the velvet bag with Mama's watch and Papa's ring, but I couldn't help it. I love to look at the shiny jewelry.

"Maggie." Someone calls. The other children are being so mean to me. I won't come out when they call, even though I can hear them running around, looking for me.

They can't find me hiding in the magnolia tree. I like to sit in the branches and listen to the wind whistle through the leaves. The other kids think the tree is haunted. They are afraid to crawl under the limbs and come into the cave-like room the branches make.

Even though they call me a baby, I'm not afraid of ghosts.

I open the cover of Mama's pretty watch with the pearl on the cover. The big hand points almost to the twelve and the little hand points to the three. Papa taught me how to tell time. It will be three o'clock very soon.

Thunder crashes over my head, and I drop the jewelry. Papa's ring hits first and the stone breaks loose. Mama's watch lands face down in the dirt. I will be in such trouble! The winds whip my hair across my face, and it stings. I scramble down the tree but I miss the bottom rung and fall on my back, knocking the breath out of me.

The storm is punishing me for taking the pouch. I get up but can't find my way from under the tree. I push through the branches as another clap of thunder brings raindrops so sharp they feel like needles on my skin. Sharp twigs tear at my clothes and try to snatch my doll, Abby, from my arms. I pull her free of the gnarly claws and we fall through the branches right as a wagon passes.

Mama calls my name but when I try to answer her, the rain splashes into my mouth and chokes me. I try to scream for her to come for me.

But something lifts me from my feet and I am pulled into a spinning tunnel.

ABOUT THE AUTHOR

 Author Allie Marie grew up in Virginia. Her favorite childhood pastime was reading Nancy Drew and Trixie Belden mysteries. When she embarked on a new vocation writing fiction after retiring from a career in law enforcement, it would have been understandable if her first book was a crime story. Researching her own family tree inspired her to write the True Colors Series instead. The other stories are patiently waiting their turn.

Her debut novel, *Teardrops of the Innocent: The White Diamond Story*, was a 2015 New England Readers' Choice Award Finalist in paranormal. The second in the series, *Heart of Courage: The Red Ruby Story* released in May 2016 and was voted Best Book in the 2017 IRC Readers' Choice Awards. February 2017 saw the release of the third book, *Voice of the Just: The Blue Sapphire Story*. The fourth book, *Hands of the Healer: The Christmas Emerald*, released in 2018. The fifth and final book in the True Colors Series will release in late fall 2018.

Besides family, Allie's passions are travel and camping with her husband Jack.

Photos by L. Somers Photography

Made in the USA
Columbia, SC
10 April 2018